YELLOW PINE

Also by Claire Vaye Watkins

I Love You but I've Chosen Darkness
Gold Fame Citrus
Battleborn

YELLOW PINE

Claire Vaye Watkins

riverrun

First published in the United States in 2026 by riverhead books,
an imprint of Penguin Random House LLC.
This edition published in Great Britain in 2026 by riverrun

an imprint of Quercus
Part of John Murray Publishing Group

1

A CIP catalogue record for this book is available from the British Library

HB ISBN 978 1 52944 972 3
TPB ISBN 978 1 52944 973 0
EBOOK ISBN 978 1 52944 974 7

Offset in 12.47/17.40pt Adobe Jenson Pro by Six Red Marbles UK, Thetford, Norfolk

Printed and bound in Great Britain by Clays Ltd, Elcograf S.p.A.

FSC
www.fsc.org
MIX
Paper | Supporting responsible forestry
FSC® C104740

Papers used by Quercus are from well-managed forests and other responsible sources.

Quercus
Carmelite House
50 Victoria Embankment
London EC4Y 0DZ

John Murray Publishing Group
Part of Hodder & Stoughton Limited
An Hachette UK company

The authorised representative in the EEA is Hachette Ireland,
8 Castlecourt Centre, Dublin 15, D15 XTP3, Ireland (email: info@hbgi.ie)

for MTM

Henceforth I travel toward Repose
—The Gospel of Mary Magdalene

YELLOW PINE

Nothingness Flats

Miles came back to Rose transformed. I mean transformed! Not a cell of him was where she'd left it. He'd fallen apart beautifully: bopped in and out of law school, then spent six years in what's left of the redwoods reading horny four-hundred-year-old poems before bailing on his PhD over a dispute with his adviser. She said he'd made no argument. He couldn't argue with that.

Rose found Miles brave and countercultural for being such a quitter. She aroused herself thinking of all the things he'd quit, first among them her, nearly two decades before. He'd been married—to the woman he left Rose for, she assumed—no, the one after her, Miles corrected—and he'd quit that too. Rose did a berserk little dance in her kitchen when she heard this. Miles's parents had also divorced, and he was not talking to his dad. Did Rose detect a patricidal shadow on his transformation? Hot.

He'd called out of the blue fog of social collapse, old fond name alight on her phone. "Well, well, well," he said when she answered. Would she care to participate in his nightly be-okay ritual, prong one of his Twelve-Pronged No Early Exits Mental Health Action Plan: Phone-A-Friend?

It was surprisingly nice to be named a friend by the man who'd once poured salt on the slug of her heart, if not Rose's top choice. She asked after his other prongs.

"Let's see: Phone-A-Friend, Gut Health, Meditation, Compassionate Inner Monologue, Walks, Solitude, Parts Work, Reparenting the Inner Child, Dream Journal, Mandatory Dance, and . . . Naps."

"That's eleven."

Miles couldn't remember his final prong.

Rose offered hers, the standard twelfth. "Having had an awakening, carry the message, practice these principles in all our affairs."

"That's three."

"Bill W.'s acid math."

"Acid is *fantastic*," Miles said. "We owe the old heads an apology about acid. Then again, they owe us a livable future. Psychedelic renaissance lifestyle brand is not gonna cut it. What's new with you? Where even are you?"

Rose told him about Nothingness Flats, a cinderblock cabin on five acres of treeless desert she'd miraculously purchased in Tecopa, a defiantly unproductive jackrabbit homestead forty miles from her childhood home.

"What's a jackrabbit homestead?"

"I'm so glad you asked." Rose had just read a book about the Small Tract Act and was crushing on its author. "The Small Tract Act was like a baby Homestead Act. Nineteen I wanna say . . . thirty-eight? Started as free housing for shell-shocked vets. Gave them five acres and the chance to build a house on supposedly worthless land. You'd order a kit from Sears, put the cabin up in a weekend."

"Some Thoreau shit."

"Precisely. Mid-twentieth-century Thoreau in the Mojave. We do not ride upon the paved road; it rides upon us kinda thing. Around Joshua Tree area mostly, Wonder Valley. Sinatra built one outside Vegas. Reagan tried but couldn't prove up."

Miles laughed. Rose saw in her mind the gap between his front teeth where they had bucked correction in his teens. "I'm serious," she said, laughing, walking outside. "He washed out down to Palm Springs!"

"That explains it." Still laughing, a miracle. "We've been stuck in Ronald Reagan's failed homesteader fantasy ever since."

"A place to heal, was the idea. Relative seclusion medicine. Taking the airs. Taking the waters."

"And have you found it to be a place of healing?"

There was the town of Tecopa and, on the other side of three hills that looked like a pregnant woman's belly and breasts, Tecopa Hot Springs, a distinction Rose could only interpret as the town's double middle fingers to civic coherence and control. Someone had climbed the two breast-shaped hills and erected big cairns in the exact placement and proportions of nipples. Hot springs seeped from the earth. Shimmering wetlands along the Amargosa River, a waterfall. The crosses here meant water, not crucifixion. "I like that."

But the county baths were closed indefinitely, and the wild nudie mud spring, a.k.a. the Borehole, was patrolled by the Bureau of Land Management, who would ticket anyone who tried to soak out there. Rose feared the famously replenishing clime long gone. She watched her expanse—its ferocious plants with their intelligent root network, its cryptobiotic crust, its cobble of patinated pebbles locking down dust since the desert was trod upon by giant ground sloths—pulverized evermore each day by bombs, mines, housing developments, data centers, so-called fulfillment centers, and industrial solar arrays. New wind—faster, stronger, hotter, longer—reaped the alkali particulate thus set loose into great toxic day-long haboobs.

"What's a haboob?"

"Dust bowl," Rose said.

"O jeez," Miles said. "Here we go again."

Rose shared more oasis woes. She let it rip. Deadpool. The lithium boom. Another gold rush in Beatty, on the headwaters of the Amargosa, sure to drain it. Grotesque agriculture subsidies—alfalfa, cotton, cattle. The evils of extraction and industrial energy. A proposed wind farm in Wee Thump, the Ancient Ones, an old-growth forest of Joshua trees and yucca and huge rare cholla stands outside Searchlight. The best campgrounds in the Mojave Preserve gentrified by Mercedes sprinter vans.

"Jesus," Miles said, "bleak."

That was not the half of it. "A million old-growth Joshua trees just burned at Cima Dome."

"What's Cima Dome?"

"It was the biggest Joshua tree forest in the world."

"Jesus," again.

San Bernardino County's wildland firefighters had been on another fire in Sequoia, wrapping General Sherman in space blankets, their backup on another fire in Oregon, their backup's backup, for reasons entirely opaque to Rose, in the Middle East.

Such was the view from Nothingness Flats. A sea of creosote swam nightly by a small clan of coyotes. Quail in their Shriner hats stressedly chortling in and out of the mesquite. Brittlebush, and the kangaroo rats who stripped them. An infinite undulation of dying basins held by rainbow mountains.

Miles asked, "How many mountains can you see from your house?"

"From where I am right now"—the gibbous moon was so bright Rose could count from her hammock—"seven ranges."

"Beautiful," Miles said.

Except on the other side of each, in every direction, was a massive military base or bombing range—Creech, China Lake, Fort Irwin, Twentynine Palms, the Nevada Test Site—installations Rose had to simultaneously hate and thank because they represented a relative wildlife refuge compared to the promised bloodbath of the coming "green-energy gold rush," and because the bombs, low-flying choppers, and late-night fireballs kept property values in Tecopa low enough that she—a nonprofit peon saddled with payment of child support and, until the heaven-sent deferments, student loans—could still afford Nothingness Flats while the tony boulder coves of Joshua Tree and the piñon shade of Pioneertown went to telecommuting coastal backwash with all-cash offers, Airbnb barons, and hedge funds. "Even Vegas is expensive now."

Thank you for your service, Rose would salute her rattling windows when the black helicopters whomped over. *Thank you for the cancer clusters, the heavy metals in the water, and for burning all that taxpayer money in the sky.*

"But have you found your people there?"

Found and lost. The Twelve-Step Club in Pahrump was a coronavirus bonanza, and Rose's Al-Anon sponsor had died of it. She'd ended things with her out-of-pocket therapist many months ago. At the time of Miles's call, Rose had not meaningfully, prolongedly interacted with another person in many months, apart from her daughter, Juniper. After an upcoming road trip to deliver June to her dad's house on the East Coast for the start of the school year, Rose was prepared to go months more. Anticipatory longing for the girl took it out of her. Pahrump, her hometown, took it out of her too. It tapped great reserves of courage to load June into the car and drive through the Resting Springs range and the Nopahs and across the Nevada state line to get groceries in the emotional minefield of her past. These days, ghoulish, permanently shocked pemmican people milled behind the Walmart, searching for a place to shit, to live, and June wanted to know why. Toilet paper Spanish-mossed the chain link and the creosotes. Deranged signs everywhere. TRUTH WINS. But whose?

Miles sighed. "It sounds like you have not found it to be a place of healing."

"Actually," Rose admitted, much to her own surprise, "I have." She'd largely thrived in isolation, a little face-starved maybe, but karmically scrubbed. Like new. "Where are you?"

In all the years since they'd split up, Rose and Miles had not wandered very far from each other, they learned, never more than one or two rain shadows away. Miles still had the van they'd traveled in together, and after dropping out of grad school, he'd lived in it around the Bay until Berkeley made sleeping in cars illegal. He did some seed harvesting up near Shasta. Some weed trimming. Taught music in juvie. Worked in a bookstore, a bar, another bookstore, a preschool. Canvassed for Marianne Williamson. Contracted on a cuckoo survey, a sage grouse survey. Woofed on a beet farm. Went up to Seattle and worked in a cheese shop before the covid dome came down and he volunteered to be laid off. Went home to Portland. "Spent most of the summer in Cully. In my mom's driveway."

"Seems like Portland was crazy this summer."

"Not crazy. Beautiful. You could commute by revolution. Every night you'd go outside for a walk and there's a few thousand other people walking with you, and every single one of them has had enough. I've never loved that city more."

"Why'd you leave?"

"Couldn't be that close to my parents. Had to bail." Since then he'd been in Truckee, camped on a buddy's back forty.

"How's Tahoe?" Rose asked.

"Tahoe's burning."

"I saw that," meaning she'd seen pictures. A video interview with a shirtless man loading up a trailer in South Lake, ash raining down and sticking to him. "He said, 'I can't believe they're gonna let the jewel burn.'"

"People are getting it," Miles said. "Tourism metaphors will not save you. Anyway, Tahoe's been over."

"Since when?"

"Since they clear-cut the forests to make mine shafts for the Comstock Lode. No, I'll tell you the day. I'll tell you the exact moment. It was this year, Fourth of July. The world's on fire, and Mark Zuckerberg rides a hydrofoil across Lake Tahoe wrapped in the American flag. You see that shit?"

Rose had not. "That's just the sort of thing I'm working on not seeing."

"Good girl," Miles said. "There's huge yachts on the lake now. There's traffic! We've always had the boats, the Jet Ski douches, but we've never had these mega yachts on the lake."

"Disgusting. You should blow them up."

"Crossed my mind, believe me. Getting the itch."

"The ecoterrorism itch?"

"Ecoterrorism's what's been done to us! The itch to split. Need a change of scenery." Miles named the ranges between them. Sierras, White Mountains, Chocolate Mountains, Inyos, Panamints, the Funeral Range. Jonesing to climb them, Rose assumed—but no, he'd quit that too. "Young man's game," he said. "But I wouldn't mind exploring those slot canyons you've got going on down there. Whole different orientation. I never did get to see your desert."

Miles estimated how long it would take to get down to Nothingness Flats in his van, said how well he had her running, how gladly he would make the journey, over which dry streams, around which drained lakes, across which blasted valleys. He said how worthy such crossings would be. Was he wanting to try again? With a troubling flutter of real hope in her heart—the sort of hope she'd jettisoned on this side of the portal, hope for the future being plainly useless in this futureless moment—Rose confessed falsely that she needed a house sitter for Nothingness Flats while she took Juniper back east, someone to water the plants and fetch the mail before it was stolen.

"I'd be honored," Miles said—reciprocity being his forgotten prong! "I could hold down the fort while you're away and shove off before you get back, if you want. Or . . ."

Rose waited, breathed, prayed.

"Or it would be great to see you again."

Rose said she'd think about it. She thought about it. She meditated on it and dreamed about it and worked the steps. She granted June unlimited screen time and sat in the sun with bentonite mud hardening on her face, sensing her way into trying again. She discerned fact from feeling. In her journal she wrote, *M needs to know that I am on this side of the portal. I have compassion in my heart for anyone back on the other side, sending emails, bickering, buying useless shit, getting run by the algorithm, living in the past. But I cannot fuck with them.*

She called him back. "You need to know that I am on this side of the portal. I have compassion in my heart for anyone stuck back on the other side, clinging to the threshold. But I can't fuck with them."

"I get it," Miles said. "Believe me. I'm on this side too. I don't care about any of that superfluous shit anymore. I deleted all my social media."

"Another thing you should know," Rose said, "is that I have *a lot* of plants, and they are very needy."

Gamely, Miles said, "Send instructions."

Instructions

So Rose wrote by hand and sent by snail mail to Miles's buddy's house in Truckee the following instructions:

Dear Miles,

Thank you for agreeing to look after Nothingness Flats and all its beings while I'm away.

First, to arrive: Don't blindly follow your phone! I don't want you to die by GPS. It won't work anyway. There's no cell service in Tecopa. If you get in a pinch, you can stop at the Triangle, where Old Spanish Trail splits around the horseshoe pits, Vegas one way, Baker another, Tecopa Hot Springs and Death Valley the third. Beside the horseshoe pits, under the salt cedars, you'll see the Giving Rock, a hunk of talc ore where we take what we need and leave what we don't. Across Old Spanish Trail from the Giving Rock is downtown Tecopa: the Kit Fox Café, the post office, the church, the Rattler Room. The bar and café are closed—for summer or for covid or for forever, I'm not sure which. Time will tell, I guess. But the Rattler Room left its Wi-Fi on, so you can park out front and download a map there. The Wi-Fi password is XXXXXXX.

My address is XXXX Arroyo Road. From the Triangle, go east on Old Spanish Trail toward Vegas. Pass the closed school and turn right, south, on Arroyo. There's no street sign, but there is a cairn of rocks where if you look close, one says Arroyo in Wite-Out. Take Arroyo for a couple miles. Pass a stand of battered mailboxes and a sign saying that this road is not maintained by the county. Pass a bottle house, a bus, a cemetery, a half-burned barn, an art-freak compound. Pass a thicket of cane grass threaded with prickly pear and junk sculptures—that's Pastor Jack, a retired schoolteacher who now preaches at the church. He's evangelical about his prickly pear, claims he grew the whole stand from one single mother plant. A greater roadrunner lives in Pastor Jack's thicket, and his cat Hambone's prone to dart, so look alive. Across from Pastor Jack is an Airbnb "casita." Egg it, if you find yourself egg-rich.

Arroyo is a rough road. I find it a helpful reframe to think of it less as a road and more as an extra-wide trail we are allowed to drive on. Pastor Jack has come up with an ingenious device, a segment of chain link weighed down by railroad ties, and he'll drag that behind his Geo periodically, a recentering ritual that must be deeply satisfying—that I-exist feeling—but does little to impact the textural chaos of Arroyo, which goes from pounding washboard to sand dune and back willy-nilly, so take it easy.

You'll pass a couple of weed farms and crest a ridge. If you downloaded a phone map, it will abandon you here, saying you have arrived when all you can see is a shredded hoop house, a capsized porta potty, and an RV with its guts spilled out. Ignore your phone.

Get out of the car and smash it with a rock. Keep driving. Descend the ridge. You'll see a slouching shed, a trampoline, then a wood plinth that says Nothingness Flats. That's me.

Originally the cabin was one cinderblock room and an outhouse. Sometime after the Tecopa Paiutes were forced onto the reservation in Moapa but before their oasis became a motel, power lines were extended down Arroyo Road, and a well was dug. Water and power combined in the swamp cooler soon thereafter added to the roof, making the place livable year-round. Granted, livability is a deeply subjective standard.

Next probably the bathroom and both bedrooms were added, making the cabin what jackrabbit homesteaders called a Biltmore. Get it? Sometime in the ghastly twentieth century, the cabin accrued telephone lines and antennae bringing TV. Next the roof accumulated three satellite dishes and, in this our even ghastlier century, two internet bringers, all of which remain up there to this very day. That's June's favorite storytelling trope: to this very day. She's seven now, old enough to know when the big wheel has turned.

Rose wrote how Pastor Jack had flipped the cabin to a group of Silver Lake vacation rental profiteers convinced Tecopa was the next Joshua Tree. The new owners added a deck, a pergola, and, though a burn ban had been in effect since time immemorial, a firepit. They painted the cabin in the mattest black they could find, lest anyone think they were from around here, and the cabin became a failed Airbnb. After several years of thwarted dreams of passive income, and at the peak of the market, the property was again put up for sale. Rose spent every penny of her savings plus an unexpected inheritance on it, almost one hundred thousand dollars.

Almost one hundred thousand dollars was a lot of money to Rose, especially considering the house was free a hundred years ago. Then again, she didn't have to get mustard-gassed to get it. The Silver Lake profiteers accepted her offer with only one peculiar condition. She was asked to surrender the house's brand: D E S E R T S T A Y.

One word, all caps, spaces between each letter.

The sellers felt they had built something with D E S E R T S T A Y, something real, something they were unwilling to relinquish. Rose agreed they could keep D E S E R T S T A Y, quipping to the unamused title officer that she wanted nothing less than to live inside a brand, and an unsayable one at that.

Rose celebrated closing on Nothingness Flats by finding D E S E R T S T A Y's Instagram. There she watched the cabin's latest transformation in reverse, from luminous minimalist "hideaway" with greige interiors, polished concrete floors, "modern appliances," and a "hammock grove," back to a dark, dingy, low-ceilinged, smoke-stained, carpeted, wood-paneled coffin. She spent no small amount of time with D E S E R T S T A Y's Instagram, her enjoyment of the house's transformation made all the more potent by not having done any of the work.

What else? Rose wrote.

> The front door likes it rough. The code is XXXX. It'll be hot when you arrive. The first thing you will want to do is turn the swamp cooler on full blast. Don't. First, crack a window. It'll feel insane, inviting the hot breath of hell inside, even just a crack, but do it. Swamp coolers need flow. Turn the dial on the wall to "pump only" to wet the pads. Takes a while (like everything worthy), but once the pads are soaked, you can crank the swamp to "hi cool" and, Goddess willing and assuming no humidity whatsoever (which in the driest place on the continent seems a reasonable assumption, but you'd be surprised in this

era of unruly atmospheric rivers) the place will be livable in no time.

As for the plants, turn on the drip lines and soak everyone outside immediately: the olive, palm, pomegranate, rosemary, beavertail, the oleanders along the driveway. Inside I've put gold stars on everyone who needs mist—please mist them promptly! Especially the depressed rubber tree near the front door and the clique of snake plants in the bedroom. They're sulky, but if treated decent will reward you with tidal waves of fresh oxygen while you sleep.

The hanging plants are openly struggling. The money tree on the big bookshelf needs a ton of affirmation. Sing to the fiddle-leaf fig, peace lily, and bird-of-paradise. The bromeliad in my bedroom is suicidal and has been for a long time—whatever happens, don't blame yourself. Drench the heart of Jesus on the toilet tank and the umbrella tree in the shower. Don't fuss over the jasmine, but don't ignore it either. June's monstera is going through something. The big aloe in the kitchen is sunburned, may have root rot, and the jade by the tub is married to its unhappiness. Same with the sago palm, and (predictably) the crown of thorns. The San Pedro needs light, more light than any one person can give. Deep soak for the elephant's ear, just a splash for the climbing philodendrons, and loving kindness for the wandering Jew.

Miles, if we are going to try again, I need everything to be different. I am going to put my mask on first, then June's. You've got to make yourself okay with that or else I'm out.

I leave a week from Friday and will be home ten days after that. If you're really on this side of the portal, I'd love to see you again. If not, you better scoot before I get back.

Yrs,

Rose

PS: Don't drink the tap water! There's a kiosk for potable water at the Triangle, by the post office, between the bulletin board and the radiation-monitoring station. Twenty-five cents a gallon.

Three days later, Miles called. "I got your instructions."

"Already?" Rose was flabbergasted. She received probably five percent of the mail sent to her at Nothingness Flats. This was George H. W. Bush's fault. One prong of Rose's own No Early Exits Mental Health Action Plan, a custom prong she'd come up with after her sponsor died, was to get an incarcerated pen pal. She signed up online, then ventured to the post office at the Triangle. She was the only one in there wearing a mask, everyone eyeballing her, especially the sassy-ass postmistress, who defied the latest research about the fallacy of multitasking by managing to give Rose a devoted stink eye while dispassionately assisting her other customers. When Rose reached the counter and asked for stamps, the postmistress slid her a booklet of George H. W. Bushes.

"All we have," the postmistress said, surely reading the top third of Rose's face and trying to get a rise out of her. Rose wanted badly to say, Really? No flowers or quilts? No glory of American aviation, no female cryptologists of World War Two? No whales, no Day of the Dead, no Pete Seegers? No butterflies, no elephants, no coral reefs, no Arnold Palmers? No flags, no *love*, no T. rexes?

Well, Rose wouldn't give the postmistress the satisfaction of conscripting her into the culture war. She accepted the Bushes with probably more grace than she'd accepted anything in her life, venting her bottomless resentment ever after by writing *War Criminal* around the stamps each time she used one. The warden did not cotton to this, apparently, for the War Criminal letters Rose sent to the prison in Indian Springs were returned to sender without fail. The mail carrier too evidently objected, for soon even the smallest packages were deemed too big for Rose's receptacle, forcing her to ride down to the Triangle to fetch them. Then the mail carrier stopped taking Rose's outgoing war criminals altogether. Between her cold war with the post office and the regular rash of mail theft with which Rose's roguish neighbors entertained themselves, her only recourse was surrender. She cultivated the belief that what mail she did get at Nothingness Flats was that which she was destined to receive. Subconsciously she assumed the same Fates culled Miles's incoming mail in Truckee, that a divine hand had delivered him her instructions, and she was awed. "Did you read them?"

"Every word," Miles said.

"And do you agree?"

"I do."

After depositing Juniper with her dad, Rose came home to a number of miracles at Nothingness Flats:

Miles's van parked beyond the plinth.

The plants thriving. Freak monsoons had the creosotes blooming in the brutal heat. Even the suicidal bromie in her bedroom was sucking out the marrow of life!

Miles. Gorgeous, lanky, unemployed, lined by time, reading Walt Whitman on her couch. Waiting, wanting Rose—wanting them—again.

What is that, five miracles?

The Portal

Rose's portal was made of creosote. It was spindly and crooked and a couple decades long. This is nothing in creosote time, but by the human clock, her portal was a long one. Rose's childhood, she and her sponsor had determined, had been one of solitude and shrewd, ferocious clinging. The only child of a poor, distant, alcoholic, and effectively single mother, Rose had spent a lot of time alone, reading or walking the mesquite dunes behind their double-wide, where wild burros came to graze. At school her desperation for attention and approval got her straight A's and a scholarship to a state school (a glorified ag college in Reno), where she fell in love with Miles and tumbled into her portal.

Unknowingly she'd envied Miles, longed to live like him, like the people in the books she studied: awake, alive, making choices, taking action, always in a story, their lives a work of art. Rose's life was not a work of art. It was not even a story. Things just sort of happened to her. A bloat of hungry, hungry hippos on Wall Street crashed the world's economy, for one, just before she graduated. Miles cheated on her. Her estranged dad, Jim, died at home in Hawai'i of cancer he'd told no one about. The bank took her mom's house, and Alice moved in with Chace, her barely literate slot-junkie boyfriend. Married him. Got deep into booze again, and Facebook. Rose could do nothing about any of this. Purely from lack of imagination, and so as not to go home, she got an expensive master's in English, specializing in literature and the environment. Alice was unimpressed. "You mastered English at the age of four."

Unlike most of the heroes and heroines in the books she loved, Rose had to have a job. Miraculously, she got one after grad school, doing "development" for the university, an excruciating euphemism, since she'd never felt more stuck. She began dating Will Álvarez, a middle-class middle school math teacher, an earthquake-safe doorjamb of a man, and egged him into marriage mainly to feel unstuck. To feel like things were moving. Like she was on the right track. Like she was the architect of her life. So many infrastructure metaphors meaning to have a baby. Rose and Will wed at the Washoe County courthouse, conceived Juniper right away, and were highly functional roommates before the baby's fontanels had closed.

It turned out there was no track, a fact Rose had to face when she reached her imagined track's terminus—Juniper Kaylani Williams-Álvarez—and had yet to meet herself. Her branchy, sun-shot portal stretched on. Fearing the day she would have to confess her mediocrity to her daughter, Rose summoned the libido to get herself a new job, the job she had presently, doing fundraising for the Mountain West chapter of the Sierra Club. During the interview, still breastfeeding, she'd been engorged with oxytocin and resolve. She'd made a being with her body, so wasn't she an architect? An artist! And weren't artists the saints of this saintless time? Rose swelled with righteousness envisioning herself working for the Sierra Club: a capable, clear-eyed helper in a culture of idiots, ostriches, and profiteers. Smugly she accepted half her development job salary and cajoled Will into relocating to Las Vegas, a place he openly considered hell. Secretly

Rose hoped that together they might stop Alice, freshly divorced and ensconced in a Pahrump trailer park an hour away, from drinking herself to death. The Sierra Club job brought Rose home, and home needed her. It had felt brave and right and pure—monkish, missionary—to go home, to go where she was needed. She would fix it, would advocate for and from the scrappy patch of wilderness that had made her, move heroically back to her barely livable region, save its river, save her mother from herself, and, with luck, salvage her rotting marriage with some free childcare.

And Rose had to admit she'd been mesmerized by her prospective boss, Topher. She'd liked that he liked her, loved that he needed her. With his movie-star jaw he declared aloud in the interview that having a state school girl from "a frontline community" writing their copy was a "geographic diversity jackpot." Rose's presence on staff (she saw now) was compensation for Topher's overenunciated mid-Atlantic accent, his actual ascots and other patrician affectations. She was a human shield, an unvoiced apology for his hereditary wealth, his joke-repeating, his excruciating icebreakers, his chronically bruised ego, his sockless loafers and the two-hundred-dollar T-shirts he wore like he didn't know how much they cost. She'd told herself the job was basically wealth redistribution, that Topher would mentor her in the ways of the rich as only a rich person could, and together they would make the bastards pay.

Now Rose knew that Topher was a mindless, self-interested impostor in way over his head. Insolent unless she instantly and aggressively validated every contradictory idea he blasted incontinently across half a dozen communication platforms. An insecure bumbler with daddy issues and likely worse, for rumors of Topher giving interns unwelcome shoulder massages and the like had wafted through the office before they'd all gone remote.

Rose knew none of this then. She had not even known she was in the portal. Yet the portal squeezed. She took the Sierra Club job and dragged her small family to Las Vegas so they might entice Alice to wellness with Will's well-meaning home-improvement projects and the regular presence of her grandchild, physical incarnation of a future worth sticking around for. If Rose delivering middle-class groceries with chunky baby Juniper on her hip—raven-haired, giant-eyed, appendages ringed with bracelets and anklets of chub—couldn't make Alice want to be here, nothing would.

Nothing would.

One night—drunk, Rose was certain—Alice fell down the back steps of her trailer. Will arrived the next morning to winterize the swamp cooler and found her on the pavers he'd installed, the back of her head mush. She was fifty-three. Rose saw then that her savior trip was far from saintly: It was an unbright child's fantasy. And she should've known better. How many gasping children had she scooped from the Pahrump town pool as a teenage lifeguard only to be screamed at by their derelict parent? We don't thank our saviors, Alice would've said. We crucify them.

Grief blew her marriage apart. Will froze, understandably. Rose was all movement, a perpetual motion machine. The shock shook something loose in her. The black-striped branches of her creosote portal rattled. She vibrated with the long-denied fact that she had not felt close to her husband in years. If ever. She could not remember the last time they'd had sex. The thought of it repulsed her. She became aware of a carapace of numbness crusted over her despairing soul. She relayed all this to Will, and he soon moved out.

When Will got a much better job back home in Philly, close to his parents and sister, Rose consented to him enrolling Juniper in preschool there. The relief she felt at Will's leaving was almost equal to the agony of being away from June two thirds of the year. She had never really respected him until he pulled that chute. Rose stayed in Las Vegas for her job, which in her reasoning was staying for the land, though she had long ago accepted that, save for some pure-heart volunteers on the Desert Committee, the Sierra Club was not especially interested in saving her unloved valley. She stayed because she was home.

The twin demolitions of death and divorce set Rose free, which was terrifying. The hours she once spent taking care of Juniper and obsessing about Alice became a chasm. Rose filled the void with program. She went to meetings, pretty much stopped drinking, did yoga religiously, started reading for fun for the first time since college, walked the desert without her phone.

She got a sponsor, Jane, seventy-five years old in a neck brace when they met and always dressed in head-to-toe athleisure wear, as if Pilates could break out at any moment and she wanted to be prepared. Jane's every appendage was adorned with sterling silver, and the bottom half of her long white hair was dyed blue as the midday sky.

"Blue is the color of consciousness," she said when Rose complimented her hair one day after a meeting. "And hair is an extension of the mind."

"What happened to your neck?" Rose asked.

"Surgery for neuropathy in my throat chakra," Jane said, "from being made to shut up as a kid. My father was a rager, always on the rampage. Little Jane went like this"—she shrugged her shoulders up and down, trying to hide in a shell she didn't have—"always having to be quiet, to make myself small. The fear made me sick."

Rose had found her sponsor.

Jane's approach to sponsorship was not exactly by the Big Book. Her methods were largely informed by her time as Ram Dass's cook at Esalen in the sixties, labor for which she'd been compensated in gestalt therapy, energy work, and other New Age trainings. "Baba Ram was a very picky eater," she told Rose, "and I was very fucked up. So it balanced out."

For the first time in her life, Rose became a dutiful daughter. She trusted Jane, did everything the woman told her to do. She read every book Jane recommended, no matter that many were not conference-approved literature: William James, Carl Jung, the Upanishads, the Taoists, a whole slew of self-help books with profoundly embarrassing titles: *The Dance of Anger. How to Talk So Kids Will Listen. How to Meditate. How to Do Nothing. How to See.*

Why was embarrassment apparently the core emotion of recovery? Was society so sick, so beyond gone collectively, that to heal at all a person had to risk ridicule? That to get a bit better raised the real possibility of being put out on the rock? Were our priorities so warped, our values so rotten, our spirits so meager, that any effort to nourish them at all was to become an object of mockery?

"Pretty much," Jane said. "We're all linked up, way down where it really matters. For the Buddha, that was good news. For us, not so much."

In her daughter's absence, Rose meditated, ate salad, scribbled honest inanities in response to the leading questions of repetitive workbooks, breathed the breathing techniques, visualized the visualizations, affirmed the affirmations, worked the work. She dumped her mother's ashes at Cathedral Canyon, and after her fourth step let the trailer park repossess Alice's trailer, mountains of shit from Rose's childhood and all. When she got the surprise call about the life-insurance payout from the culinary union, Rose considered it her Higher Power's unsubtle shove into the wilderness—three-hour round-trip commute be damned!—and bought the cabin two ranges west, just across the California state line in Tecopa, a place her mother had loved.

When covid came, Rose found herself amazingly well suited to quarantine. How freeing, how illuminating (in a deeply sad way) to watch pointless obligations slough off like so much dead skin. Circle-ups, brainstorming sessions, Kabuki stakeholder meetings, wonky luncheons, excruciating conferences in DC, obscene galas in LA and New York, her spine-pulverizing commute—Rose mourned none of it. Only admonished herself for spending so much of her precious life doing things she hated with people she didn't even know.

Then Jane died.

Alone, Rose molted. The creosote branches of the portal squeezed, snagged on the last shreds of her carapace. She shimmied, shucked, stopped responding to Topher and "the team" on all but one of the communication platforms and never outside of work hours, which she silently adjusted from nine to five to eleven to two. She started waiting a full day before replying to Topher's freak-outs, at which point the alleged emergency had always resolved itself. She nested at Nothingness Flats, planted, painted, walked the canyon, prayed, meditated, read, lurked in Al-Anon meetings online, did yoga online, FaceTimed with Juniper, sent the girl postcards and flowers and presents, received her on breaks and then let her go again.

Which made Rose think of George Floyd calling for his mother. Of the girl who'd filmed it. Of courage. Of saints. Of Miles in Portland tear-gassed nightly by the state. Of protesters snatched into unmarked vans. Of Pastor Jack, who stood in front of the Shell station in Pahrump on Fridays holding two signs, one old, one new. The cardboard of his old sign was warped, its faded letters barely readable: NO SACRIFICE ZONES. His other sign was fresh, for he remade it every week, smooth cardboard presenting in black marker Shell's latest record profits.

By way of welcome to the neighborhood, Pastor Jack invited Rose to join him there on Fridays. Once, she did. She supposed it took courage to be there, standing in her mask as trucks emblazoned with neo-Nazi insignia and nut sacks dangling off their hitches gunned their engines with such raging animus that she sincerely expected them to jump the curb and plow her down, as it was newly legal to do. But she didn't feel courageous. She didn't feel saintly. Mostly she felt embarrassed.

Yet there were moments there in front of the Shell when she felt intensely alive. Alight. An enormous engine roared at her from inside its gleaming waxed shield of sculpted steel, the word *RAM* coming at her in chrome, and Rose was lit from within. Ready. On the sidewalk she took a small, barely perceptible step forward. Eyes closed and finally seeing, she emerged from the portal.

Don't threaten me with a good time.

When the murderous Ram and its triggered driver had passed, Rose opened her eyes. Pastor Jack stared at her. What he said was, "You ever heard of Yellow Pine?"

Bagging Peaks

Rose and Miles sallied forth, trying again in Indian summer in a low-key failed state on a dying planet. They woke in each other's arms to the smell of smoke, found the rainbow mountains around them deleted and the sky an incorrect color. Miles made coffee while Rose checked the Cal Fire website, mesmerized by the fire icons in every direction. He nudged her phone with a steaming mug. "Mind your dosage."

The news was bad, but Miles was the best distraction. Rose's standard miasma of sorrow and rage shimmered now with golden joy. He was even more beautiful than she'd remembered—bafflingly gorgeous, perfect proportions, every angle begging to be painted or kissed. And so moist! He was such a carnal magnet for Rose that she struggled to focus on the brilliant, bonkers ideas off-gassing from his brain. She got lost in the lines of him, his radiance and coloring, her fingers probing the dark forest of his wild, unwashed hair. She surveyed his weather-softened skin, his feathery eyelashes, their sun-bleached tips, the watershed of veins coursing down his forearms and hands, his long fingers and long, unhurried dick. She wanted him all the time, desire surging through her at unprecedented rates, in unprecedented shapes—her new weather. And when she did listen to him and managed to grasp some meaningful percentage of what he said—forget it!

Rose loved the world better through Miles's eyes. A lizard commuting between creosotes made him vibrate with wonder. He found genuine pleasure in the feel of a sturdy water glass, licked rocks to see their true colors. He was brilliant, peaceful, grounded as a mountain, kind even when he was blue, an unabashed loner agog at the whole burning world. "Every mouse a miracle," he said when they found the toilet paper stockpile in the pantry shredded, the wires on Rose's car newly gnawed.

Rose did not want to spook Miles, but she was falling for him again with frightening velocity, even faster than last time. The prudent part of her went, *No, no, no, no, no, absolutely not, not again!*

And the unafraid part replied, *Noted and disregarded.*

Love laid down a new layer. Rose's despair patinaed with faith. Where once she scurried about anxious as an ant, keeping her Prius loaded with water and nonperishables, homesick for the time before she knew there was such a thing as the Air Quality Index, she now bounced through her prepping rituals like a bird, her spirits kettling high above every noxious plume, surfing the starry current of new love.

Was it new love? Or old love rekindled? Had Rose been in love with Miles the whole time they'd been apart? She often thought so. So did she love him still, or love him again? Maybe she loved him for the first time, since last time around they never did say it.

However Rose parsed it, the feeling was naked, total, a love that blotted out the sun. She rode the brakes as long as she could and then, almost a month in, the heat broke and the smoke cleared, and like an idiot Rose told him.

They were out on the first hike the AQI allowed them, to the Amargosa Canyon. Rose took Miles on what was once the Tonopah and Tidewater line, before its rails were ripped up for the war effort. *The town was on a dry river bed between Death Valley and the Nevada line.* Joan Didion wrote that. But here in the canyon the river flowed. *There were two trees in the town, two cottonwoods in the dry river bed, but one of them was dead.* Both the cottonwoods were dead now, but no matter. Joan's Maria visited Tecopa in the mining-and-cattle era. Miles and Rose enjoyed the wild-and-scenic-river era. No more cottonwoods, but willows, cattails and tule, grapevines, brittlebush, sagebrush, beavertail, rare fish-smelling niterwort, a cluster of three stately palms. Hanging gardens and waterfalls. With enough rain, they'd have wildflowers.

Miles and Rose held their breath at two cottontails flushed from a stand of mesquite. They stood in astonishment as an annoyed coyote made its way goatlike up the hanging gardens. They flirted and ambled, Miles smelling everything. Walking with him was like walking with a dog or a toddler—nothing too ordinary for his devotion. He stopped at a massive stand of ancient and decadently fragranced trees Rose knew he would love.

"Desert willow," she said. Working for the Club, she'd had to learn the names of things.

"Not technically willow," Miles observed. "Bignonias."

"Begonias?"

"Bignonias. *Chilopsis linearis.* Begonias are rose clade. These are mint clade. Two totally different clades. Learned that from these botanists I worked under."

"Good to know," Rose said, feeling dumb.

"Is it?" Miles said harshly. "I actually hate that I said that. That's the problem with science. Not just it's arrogant. Smug. It's hostile to actual existence. Indifferent at best. It cuts everything up. How is the distinction between rose clade and mint clade helpful for experiencing these trees? For knowing them? For loving them? What does that way of knowing offer anyone?"

"Say the Latin again."

"No."

Rose wrapped her arms around his narrow waist, looked up at him, with her eyes said please.

Miles kissed her forehead. "*Chilopsis linearis,*" he whispered.

Together they sauntered down a wash to the skinny chocolate milk river and leapt over it. On the other side, they jagged up out of the riverbed, Rose leading Miles to her regular route, a path appearing on no maps, long-forgotten wagon ruts running up Mount Tecopa.

"There's a cool mine up there. Insane views. But we don't have to get to the top. I've seen it a bunch."

"Fine by me," Miles said. "I'm not about bagging peaks. More process-oriented these days."

Rose asked why.

He shrugged. "At a certain point I had to ask myself why I need to be dangling off El Cap without a rope to feel the presence of God."

"You didn't—"

"I did."

"That's madness," she said. How could he be so careless with himself when she loved him so? "Why would you do that?"

"I told you," Miles said, "for God. It was like meditation. The way it focuses you. You can't think of anything else but your body and the rock. It brings you back to your body. You feel everything. The wind, your breath. It makes you in the world. And gets you out of yourself? The world could be ending down below and it doesn't matter. I was sort of getting off on it, I think."

"On death?"

"Hell yeah! Death is sexy. You get it. You wouldn't be out here if you didn't get it. You're brave. Messianic time turns you on. It makes us feel special, to have made it to the end, no matter how ghastly we think the end will be. There's something freeing about having the exit in sight."

They climbed quietly awhile. People often said Rose was brave when they learned what she did for work, brave and good. Once, she might have agreed. But these days she felt like a flunky for the nonprofit-corporate-industrial complex, a whipper of frenzy, a vulture, an opportunistic bottler of rage, a hack alchemist attempting with shrieky, automated, and largely ignored emails to transform grief into cash. A miner of fear.

She thought of a line of Flannery O'Connor's. "*She would of been a good woman,*" she told Miles, "*if it had been somebody there to shoot her every minute of her life*. The Misfit said that."

Miles blinked. "I don't need that anymore," he said. "To feel alive. To know my own goodness. Now I just . . . read. Walk. Look about me. Trying to be more Whitman than Muir. I've heard what the talkers are talking. Now I can just . . ." He snapped his fingers. "Turn it on."

Slowly they did bag the peak. "Death *is* sexy," Rose admitted at the top. "That's probably why we're so okay with mass extinction."

"Loss makes you feel alive," Miles said, staring down through an iron grate into the dark throat of the mine. "Maybe there's nothing wrong with that."

"It feels wrong," Rose said. "Seven million people just died."

"Same as die from air pollution every year."

"That's what I'm saying. We need to grieve. To mark the loss." She told him about the Shell scene, Pastor Jack's signs, the wrathful duallies of Pahrump. She told him about Yellow Pine, an industrial solar array under construction in at the south end of the Pahrump Valley, one range east of Tecopa, grinding up yucca and creosote forest, evicting tortoises, crushing their babies, about the protest camp Pastor Jack had invited her to join. "It's not a blockade," she said. "We're not delusional. It's more of a vigil. Mourning the land as we knew it."

"Though we hardly knew it."

"I knew it," Rose said. "It raised me. You know it. You know your clades."

"Clades," Miles scoffed, tossing a rock. "I don't want to know like that anymore." He took her hand. Rose did not know what way of knowing he preferred, what other ways there were to choose from.

They skittered down the mine tailings, settled in for a picnic near the remnants of a miner's shack—crumbling adobe bricks, peels of corrugated tin the color of dried blood. They went on trying to feel the pain rippling across the world. It had everything to do with settler colonialism, was Miles's thesis, the American West's enforced amnesia. The unmarked carnage, the blood-soaked soil, the festering denial. "We lost the land's long memory. We lost the ideas cocreated with this place."

"Memory's tricky," Rose said. She'd often felt trapped in hers. And what good had that done? "It's not 1848." Pilfering Wallace Stegner, Rose observed that they were not Europeans, did not look to Europe. And wasn't citizenship more than time? Her roots in this desert were nothing in Turtle Island time, true, but could there not be some wisdom in them? Some detox from imperial insanity, some chance for . . . what? *Peace?* Dicey ideas she daren't air elsewhere. "We have to recover from tree culture."

"This from a person who named her child Juniper!" laughed Miles. "I'm of tree culture. There's tree culture here. Piñon pine? The flipping bristlecones!"

"Those are trees, not tree *culture*."

"What about the sky islands?" Miles cried. "But I get it. I'm picking up what you're putting down. Tree worship didn't translate down here. You can't just import the druid thing and expect it to be a cogent spirituality."

"That's where the homesteaders went off the rails," Rose said. "Mandatory trees. Enforced improvement. Too rooted. Stegner said movement was the defining force of the American West. Movement and aridity. He talked about being a placed rather than a displaced person. Maybe we have to be both."

"If we're going to stay here, we have to get good at leaving."

Rose didn't like the sound of that, but she tried acceptance. "Root to rise," she said, then when Miles looked mystified, "Some yoga shit."

There were supposed to be something like a billion climate refugees by 2050, Miles said. "If we're not among them, we're going to be receiving them." It was a paradox, he said, to hunker down, they had to be uprooted. Lucky were the nimble, they decided. Lucky were those who would pass through this global portal intact and live long enough to watch the land called the American West burn. The question was how. All they had to do, the lovers agreed, was end the United States and with whatever was born in its aftermath reexamine every given—electricity, housing, property, health care, policing, transportation, work, family, money, war—until everyone had the tools of adaptability and resilience presently enjoyed by the rich.

"Like multiple homes," Miles said. "And borderless migration."

A bad cloud had materialized to the east. "A new one," Rose said.

"Where?"

She pointed. "Over Mount Charleston." The origin of the world, she'd learned at Yellow Pine.

Miles groaned. They watched the smoke bruise the sky, tried to name its color. Burnt red? Copper? "Some yellow-green in there," Miles said.

"Like a penny dipped in some awful forever chemical."

"Creepy."

Take fire, Miles said. Suppose we thought fire something to live with, not war against. They agreed it pure hubris to deploy the same methods of aggression and exploitation that caused climate collapse to fix it. They clucked their tongues and cursed this doubling down on the warmonger's logic, the racket that hardened borders and militarized the police to protect industry and property over people and the planet.

"I read this article somewhere," Rose said, tucking into a peanut butter and jelly sandwich from her backpack, "about privatized firefighting, about fire contractors getting rich and paying poverty wages to the guys who actually go out there and risk their lives. I mean, they're basically gig workers."

"Along with the prisoners."

Did he know they were not letting their families visit them at base camp anymore?

"Because of covid?"

Rose nodded maniacally. She hadn't had anyone to talk to like this in a long time. Maybe since last time. The article had quoted an anonymous firefighter. "He said—I keep thinking about it—he said, 'It's a little bit of a Halliburton situation.'"

"Those *fuckers.*" Miles cracked open two cans of beer from his backpack and handed one to Rose.

Rose took it, with her other hand whirled her sandwich up into the air like a dust devil, going on about Halliburton and the like. "They don't care if these catastrophes compound."

"They need them to compound," Miles said, slurping foam. "The rich get richer while the rest of us roast."

Rose swigged; she raved. When the mountains burn, let their myths burn too. Which myths? The myths of the American West!

The rugged individual conquering nature. Looking at the land and thinking God wants you to take it. Manifest destiny. The whole genocidal, ecocidal land grab disguised as spiritual wholeness.

"O," Miles laughed, "those."

They ate and drank awhile in quiet. Surveying the vast valleys below, Miles tried to get his bearings. Rose showed him the borders of the national park.

"America's best idea," Miles said acidly. "More like a big zoo."

"And these days you have to wonder to what extent our 'best' idea enabled our worst ideas." She jabbed her chin beyond Death Valley, toward Yucca Mountain and the Nevada Test Site, the most bombed place on earth, range after range, basin after basin, sky island after sky island sacrificed to the most prolific polluter on the planet.

Miles munched puzzledly his PB&J. "I don't get it."

"I don't know," Rose said. "Sometimes I think, like, maybe setting aside some land—and I'm not saying this is what John Muir was after—Roosevelt, maybe, probably—"

"That fucking guy—"

"Maybe setting aside these little patches of special land, making them national parks, maybe that made it possible for us to completely ruin the rest of the planet. It gave us a false sense of security. Fake peace. It separated things into two categories: worthy and unworthy."

"Killable, not killable."

"A sort of tokenism?" said Rose. "A pressure-relief valve? A permission structure?"

"That's what I think about when I hear about these 'wildlife connectivity corridors.' Like, what does that make everything else? An office park? One big strip mall?" Miles looked east, away from the park. "You can see Nothingness Flats from here."

Rose found it, found Pastor Jack's thicket, the casita, the wacky art compound called Villa Anita, the cemetery, the Triangle down the hill, the springs and wetlands threaded through it all like sargassum smeared at the bottom of the long-gone ice age ocean. She felt a familiar psychic whinge behind her breastbone.

Miles touched her elbow as if to say, What is it?

"I feel this whiplash out here." Pointing to the park, she said, "God's country." She flipped her hand around roughly in the direction of Yellow Pine. "Sacrifice zone. I wonder where I fall on this spectrum. June and me."

"Hey, Siri," Miles said into his palm, "where is Nothingness Flats on the national killability index?"

Rose laughed. There was so much more laughter on this side of the portal than she thought there would be. But the laughter loosed in her more sadness. "Sometimes I think I can feel the planet just hemorrhaging under all this greed. Like it's tectonic. Like greed's a force of nature. But it's not."

"It's *not*," Miles confirmed.

"A park is a decision," Rose said. "A base is a decision."

"And a budget is a moral document," Miles said. "The US military could be refashioned as a peaceful climate corps tomorrow if we want it."

They swigged the last of their beers and stewed awhile, silent in their helplessness, their excess safety and inescapable complicity, Rose assumed. Then Miles stood to repack his bag. "Getting hot," he said, taking her empty can. He stomped it, tucked it gingerly into a mesh pouch on his backpack.

"You want to recycle those?" Rose asked. "We can stop by the county bin."

Miles shrugged. "Why not? I try not to overdo it with the personal responsibility hogwash, but what the hay?" Poised to stomp his own can, Miles stopped, his fiery eyes alight with idea. He gestured to the scraps of rusted tin beside them, then up to the mine. "You know what I think?" he said. "I think these things are connected."

"Very astute, time detective."

"Yep." He stomped his can, stowed it, nodded. "Something definitely happened here."

"But more important," Rose said, "something didn't." She pointed to the yucca colony near where the shack had been, spiky explosions of bright-green tines spearing up from shaggy brown bodysuits of dead ones.

"What a beaut," Miles said. "*Yucca . . . schidigera?*"

Rose shrugged. "Spanish dagger. Cousin of the Joshua tree."

He got close to the plant, squatted down beside it, peered at the tidy holes bored in. "Who lives here?"

"Everyone," Rose told him. "Birds. Owls. Kangaroo rats. Desert night lizards."

Miles fondled the plant's withered brown tines, examined its largest crown, a spray of spears flung back as if frozen mid-headbang. He stood and brought his palm to the tip of one of these exuberant spikes—druid madness.

"Don't touch!" Rose cried as Miles said "Ouch" and recoiled. They both inspected his bloodless palm.

Rose showed him the babies poking up through the yucca's husk skirt. "It looks like one plant, but it's actually a few generations all growing on top of each other."

Miles gawked fondly. "*The smallest sprout shows there is really no death.*" Some Whitman he'd read her that morning.

"Everything out here grows so slow," Rose said. "Once you realize how slow, it all becomes a miracle."

"*To die is different from what anyone supposed,*" Miles said, "*and luckier.*"

"You're really on a Whitman kick."

"It's wild to read someone who thinks this country is a good idea. He seems useful for the postmortem. Figuring out what scraps to salvage."

"I think about that, up here," Rose said.

"Think about what?"

"Salvage. I think how old this yucca family is. Easily hundreds of years. It was definitely here in the mining days. Through the booms. And see how it's the only one up here?"

Miles surveyed the mountainside and concurred.

"I bet there were more once," Rose said. "Before the mine. Could have been a forest of them. We don't know."

Miles put his arms around her from behind and squeezed. "You use that word pretty liberally, *forest*."

"I sure do." Rose took his hand, kissed his poked palm, openly worshipping his skin. *I have felt other good skin, but this skin is just the edge of something else.* Lydia Davis said that. Rose gestured beyond the tin scraps to the mine. "There probably was a yucca forest up here. Like the one at Yellow Pine. Just yesterday in geologic time. *Today* in geologic time!" She'd been reading John McPhee. "The geologic present."

Miles said, *"I do not talk of the beginning or the end."*

Rose had no idea what that meant. "What's important," she said, "what I try to remember—is this one, *this* yucca family is here *now*. Still here. Right by this camp. Right next to where the miners lived. In their front yard pretty much." When they'd moved out to Tecopa, June said, "We used to have a yard but now we just have land."

"They—" Rose said.

"Who?"

"The miners. They would've walked by this yucca countless times every day, cooking on a fire, working their claim. They saw it out their window every morning."

"Assuming they had a window."

"They could have cut it down at any point. Anyone could have. Anyone could have come along, any day—pushed it over at any *moment*! But they didn't. It's here because they *didn't*."

"No one did."

"Exactly," Rose said. "Most people don't. The vast majority of people are not hell-bent on destroying every living thing on the planet, not actively accelerating the devastation, not trying to peace out to Mars."

Miles laughed. "You're not going to Mars?"

"Fuck no! And I can't wait for everyone who wants off this planet to leave."

"The Mars scene'll be bad," Miles said. Behind him, the wildfire smoke had arranged itself in layers, tiers descending the Spring Mountains toward Las Vegas. "A handful of super-rich psychopaths who don't know the difference between experience and representation. Good riddance. The trick is to stop them from wrecking this place on their way out."

"There are more of us than there are them," Rose said. "I've been trying to remember that." It was about all she'd been doing. The scale of the loss was staggering. And pretty much permanent. But being carried out by a tiny fraction of people. A group of people who could fit inside a large conference room. She'd spent no small amount of time envisioning the room. "The vast majority of us mean no harm."

"Praise be," Miles said, and gave her a deep, resuscitating kiss. He plunged his tongue to her bare-stript heart. Whitman said that.

It was then, heart bare-stript and dumb with luck, that Rose told him. It was folly, she knew—too soon! too fast! too much!—but she had to.

When they came up for air she said, "I love you."

Miles smiled, his perfect face alight under the jaundicing sky.

"I'm in love with you," Rose said stupidly.

"I know," he said, leaning down and smooching her third eye. "I'm so glad."

That's fine! Rose screamed inside herself walking down the mountain. *I am a grown-ass woman surrendered to her Higher Power and practiced in the art of self-soothing. For the first time in my life, I enjoy my own company. He loved me before. He'll love me again.*

Halfway down the mountain, they paused for water and observed the smoking section of the sky. Miles predicted that the sunset would be spectacular. "Maybe," he said as they recrossed the muddy trickle of river, "if we could feel this suffering, look at it, sit with it, maybe we would learn from it. Correct our mistakes. Lord knows I'm no expert, but I think that's how healthy growth is supposed to go."

Rose said the world needed to mourn collectively, having no idea what that would look like. But wasn't it the only way to move through the pain and rage and make some better decisions? Build a social safety net? Not that this seemed likely. He had promised elegy, to be a bridge—had offered these in exchange for revolution—but now the new president was saying quit the malarkey and get back to work.

"Fuck a social safety net," said Miles. He wanted a social canopy, an on-purpose society that honored the land, gave it rights. No, fuck rights, he revised, scrambling over a sparkling boulder. Rights were a big mistake. No being needs the state's permission to exist.

He took her hand and pulled her out of the wash. He looked into her eyes and smiled. Words or no words, Rose felt loved by him. She felt his lovelight warm as the sun. "We claim we worship this land," she said, "so let's worship it."

"That's the problem," Miles said, "with this time. With 'in this house we believe.'"

"Fear is the mind killer."

"The aggressive rationalization. 'Believe science.' That's not how science works. It's not how belief works! We don't know how to worship anymore. We don't know how to pray."

Rose agreed, interpreting *we* as *they*. Because if *we* don't know how to pray, then what have *we* been doing?

Prayer

Pastor Jack had taken Rose out to Yellow Pine the first time. He picked her up in his Chinook, humped like a tortoise over the steering wheel, watery eyes excited, unmasked, dentures gleaming. She thought, *Okay,* and left her mask in her pocket but kept her window down. He seemed older here, piloting the Chinook, than he had in front of the Shell. His knobby hands trembled and looked like they hurt. Over the creaking of the RV as it efforted up into the mountains on Old Spanish Trail, he told her about the girlfriend of one of his parishioners as if she was a friend they had in common. A twenty-two-year-old woman who'd overdosed the day before. "Left two kids," he said. "Beautiful little girls."

"Terrible," said Rose. "How old?"

"Four and six. They found her."

What was anyone supposed to do with that? In her head Rose said the serenity prayer. She asked God to look after those girls, knew this worse than nothing. She should have told the pastor to turn around and take her to those kids so she could scoop them up. He turned up the volume on the tape deck. Lucinda Williams. The Chinook gurgled up the pass. As they approached the hairpin turn at the summit, where Old Spanish Trail swung wide to the edge of craggy volcanic cliffs, Rose prayed he would slow down. Then she said, over Lucinda, "Can you go slower?"

"Why sure," Jack said, and slowed.

"Please," Rose said. "Thank you." She relaxed a little. They rounded the turn, and the south Pahrump Valley expanded vastly beneath them, almost untouched save for the road they were on and, to the north, the town of Pahrump, from here just a dappling of dusty gray structures on the far side of the dry lake bed.

There were energies waiting for Rose in this valley, people she could not see any more than she could see the invisible lines where California became Nevada, where Nye County became Clark County, the arbitrary jurisdictional geometry that put Yellow Pine up for sacrifice.

Juniper was in the valley, wanting to know why. June was safe, Rose told herself, her be-okay mantra. June was well cared for, she was with the other best person for her, and that person and Rose had chosen to live on opposite sides of the continent, a freedom neither of them wanted to surrender nor wanted the other to have to surrender. Unless they intended to yank June back and forth between schools for the rest of her childhood (an arrangement their low-budget mediator said family court was unlikely to accept) one of them got to be the school-year parent and the other one got her on breaks. That other one was currently Rose. She'd volunteered because someone had to, because she'd been sopping with guilt when the decision needed making, and because she could bear it.

The dead waited too, though Rose did not yet know it. Her parents. Her sponsor, Jane, whom Rose had loved as she had never dared to love her own mother. What Rose did see, dropping into the south Pahrump Valley in Pastor Jack's Chinook, was a creosote sea gold in the late light. Huge alluvial plains sloping up to plum and lavender mountains shadowed with wedges of indigo. The time-shaved Kingstons to the south, a dead mine gashed in them, identifiable by its upchuck of tailings.

Pastor Jack turned down the music. "All this used to be a lake, you know."

Rose knew. "Like ten thousand years ago."

The Old Spanish Trail. Did she know why it was called that? She did but he went on. Old trail the Spanish used to use. For horses. To get their horses to the coast. To sell them. "Eighteen-twenties," he said. "Took twelve weeks." Pastor Jack quizzed her on the water stops along the trail. Mountain Springs, Stump Springs, Resting Springs, Chapo Springs, Tecopa Hot Springs. "Course Stump Springs is dry now."

"Chapo too," said Rose. A sad fact she'd gleaned from a flame war between rival hydrologists on the Club LISTSERV.

"You know it all!" he said. Rose heard "know-it-all" and shriveled. The pastor kept on blabbing. Did she know why they came so far out of the way, the Spanish? On a route with such bad water, when there's a shorter and perfectly pleasant route south through Needles? He twitched his gnarled right hand toward Arizona. "Much more convenient to go along the Colorado and cross at Fort Mojave. Know why they didn't?"

Rose admitted she did not.

"Because there was no Fort Mojave then!" he rejoiced. "The fort popped up after, because of what happened. The Spanish had to come through here because the Mojaves were killing everyone who tried to cross down there."

"Everyone?"

"Everyone!" In fact a few people. The Mojave had ambushed a

party of traders coming down the river with their families. "Some of their people had been killed."

Quite a few, Rose imagined.

"So they'd had enough," he said. "Told the Spanish to take a hike. So they hiked here!"

Rose had driven this section of the Old Spanish Trail countless times on her way to and from Las Vegas. She knew every pothole and swept-away segment of shoulder. As a teenager she'd driven to this end of the valley with boyfriends to do donuts across the splendidly white dry lake bed. Once she'd gotten stuck in the playa's surprise mud and had to trudge all the way to the brothel on the outskirts of Pahrump to use their phone. She knew the gravel pit, the Joshua tree forest upslope off Highway 160, knew the dune bosque where Stump Springs had been. She recoiled from the cursed grow ops and puppy mills of Charleston View, puzzled at the confusing stucco monastery–rest stop, always closed, loathed the turnoff to a sizable firing range ("tactical training resort") boasting bazookas and Uzis. She clocked the blue glass pyramid of Soul Banya, A RUSSIAN STEAM HOUSE, its hand-painted sign said, and across from that the earth domes of 3 Moons, a natural building compound led by an exuberant Belgian CalEarth apostate in her nineties. From her job, Rose knew the government's hidden districts, how the land on the California side of the state line was semiprotected by the Desert Renewable Energy Conservation Plan (DRECP) but the same habitat on the Nevada side was a designated leasing area (DLA). She ached toward Cathedral Canyon, the box canyon where she'd gone with her mom to AA roundups and where Rose had spread her ashes. The psychedelically striped mountains to the west were the Nopahs. To the east, the Spring Mountains sat immovable as a buddha with robes spread between Pahrump and Las Vegas. Their benevolent peak, Mount

Charleston, was one of the highest in the Mojave, and from the Pahrump side seemed leaned in subtle repose, watching.

"Look at that," Pastor Jack said to the summit before them.

Rose looked. The mountain's crown was flecked with a few astonishing slugs of snow. "Who was Charleston anyway?"

Pastor Jack shrugged. "Don't know him. We live in a special place. Nevada. Know what that means?"

"Snowy," said Rose, feeling about eight.

"That's right!" Surely Pastor Jack was not this naïve to the intensity with which Nevada's schoolchildren are indoctrinated with state trivia? "Snowy mountains."

"Just snowy," said Rose. The original name proposed at statehood, Sierra Nevada, described all the mountains across the entire territory, from Lake Tahoe to Salt Lake. "They cut off the *mountains* in DC. Kind of crazy when you think about it. The driest state in the union called snowy. Snowy what? Snowy nothing." *Sierra Nevada* had shrunk to mean just the one range, a range not even mostly in Nevada, a range everyone worshipped. Which, fine, she said—but they all deserved worship.

Pastor Jack dipped his head in fake interest and turned up Lucinda.

Rose thought she knew this valley, but she had never noticed the place where Pastor Jack pulled over a couple of songs later, the place he called Yellow Pine. Yellow Pine, he explained, was a new name given by NextEra Energy—a Florida energy conglomerate valued at $175 billion—to a five-thousand-acre trapezoid of formerly public land. The solar array then was nothing more than a sparse line of wooden stakes hammered into the dirt and tied with strips of fluorescent-pink plastic flapping in the breeze. They got out of the RV and followed the stakes to a teardrop trailer wedged near a

Subaru. From the teardrop (plainly handmade, mostly of wood) a strange and glorious creature emerged: a scantily clad goddess with a lizard head, dancing. This was Fran, founder of Camp Yellow Pine, though what Pastor Jack murmured was, "O Lord."

Fran was quite fetching, Rose realized when she removed her lizard mask and introduced herself. An ecofeminist Whitmanic poetess of equine bearing on hiatus from her PhD at UNLV, she'd been living at Yellow Pine since the array's initial application was approved. She offered to give Rose the tour.

Pastor Jack stayed at camp—bad knees—while Fran and Rose walked the site in the late-day sun. Enormous and insistent, the sun at that crazy-making end of afternoon angle blinded every westward gaze. It was the time of day that makes you pray rashly for the sun to go down and never come up again, an ocular agony that somehow every day eventually resolved into the prismatic bliss of sunset. But the sun had not relented yet, the ancient and winsome yucca colonies shining with supernatural stamina, the creosote rings haloed. Fran was on Rose's left, westerly and backlit to oblivion, so Rose heard without seeing her as they walked. In this way, what the lizard woman horse poet said seemed to come from the plants themselves, from the lichen and fungi, from the underground root network of bacterial crusts and invisible microbes.

"Five thousand acres of pure spirit," Fran called the place. It was obviously true, even if one was unaware that, as an elder named Matt would later explain in a speech at a campout, Mount Charleston, according to the Salt Songs, the Chemehuevi's mythic ceremonial song cycle, was the place where people began. It was like Nuwu Mount Olympus. A woefully Western analogy, Fran conceded. Still, it would have been a big help during Rose's gothic childhood "over the hump in Pahrump the dump" to know she was in fact coming of age at the foot of the origin of the world.

Fran's reverence was novel to Rose. A little embarrassing, but stirring too. It was the first time she had heard her home valley regarded with anything other than fear poorly masked by sneering contempt. In Fran's telling, this patch preposterously called Yellow Pine (not a pine for a hundred miles) was a drought-withered, suffering, yet resilient, intact and very alive sacred place that NextEra, in cahoots with Warren Buffett's NV Energy (Rose heard "Envy Energy"), was hell-bent on pulverizing for a profane amount of profit. A criminal amount of profit. Until very recently Yellow Pine was public land, the commons. As fraught a notion as that was on a stolen continent, they could not allow the unslakable thirst of rich men to fuel the engines that would turn the wheels that would crush the living cryptobiotic crust unfurled across the land like clumps of crusty velvet. The machines—already waiting on the shoulder of Highway 160—would scrape away the ancient, delicately interlocking stones geologists called desert pavement, an intricate formation of rocks millions of years in the making, sending up a tremendous slo-mo explosion of toxic dust.

But first, the tortoises. There were hundreds of endangered desert tortoises living at Yellow Pine, Fran said. When tortoise habitat became solar array, the Endangered Species Act mandated that adult desert tortoises be transplanted from the site—"mitigated," in the banal-evil lexicon of the Bureau of Land Management, meaning shoveled up from their burrows and moved out of the path of rampaging greed. Tortoises were not intrepid travelers. They spent the entirety of their long lives in one small, intimately memorized patch of desert maybe a mile square. Few tortoises survived mitigation. Tortoise numbers were plummeting. The desert tortoise, Fran said, was being mitigated into extinction.

What really got Rose was how they died. The evicted tortoises always came back. Slowly, but with their famed steadiness, the displaced tortoises went home. Or they tried. They returned looking for their burrows, for where they'd always found food, for the exact spot where they scratched a certain groove in the dirt to gather dew. They came looking for their mates, for their babies. But instead of home, sustenance, or love, the tortoises would come up against a "tortoise exclusion fence" that would soon replace the pink-flagged stakes now delineating the Yellow Pine site. An adult tortoise would scrape slowly alongside the tortoise exclusion fence for miles, circumnavigating the site until it died.

The juvenile and baby tortoises of Yellow Pine would fare no better. They were too small for contractors to find and relocate within the timeline demanded by construction, so they'd be left behind to be crushed by graders, excavators, bulldozers, backhoes, cutting machines, end loaders, and water trucks. And for what? Fran said. Yellow Pine's electricity was destined for something called the Silicon Valley Electric Authority. For data centers, for a so-called cloud that was in fact metals and minerals, water and emissions. All so the earth's affluent could find every email they'd ever written?

It wasn't enough to be anti, Fran knew. You had to be for something. The alternative to greed-drunk investor-owned utilities, she said, was free distributed community solar in the built environment and on disturbed lands. They were desert rats for an energy commons. They wanted publicly owned panels put up over parking lots, military bases, golf courses that never should have been there in the first place, dried alfalfa fields and other busted ag land made increasingly antediluvian each day the Colorado River dropped closer to dead.

Their demand was simple: Put solar in the cities first, where most of the energy was used, and where environmental policy was more palatable, rather than the cowardly "all of the above" approach the current administration endorsed with cover from the Club. To kill this land, to turn open public wilderness into an industrial alley, aside from being wrong, would surely drive the people who lived out here into deeper alliance with climate deniers and violent fascists. Fran preached the necessity of rejecting the false choice between transitioning off fossil fuels and protecting biodiversity, a wedge easily cleaving what was left of American environmentalism. True. Every day at work, in the subcommittees and on the LISTSERVs, Rose watched it put the cloistered cottontops of the movement at each other's throats.

Fran led Rose back to camp as the Nopahs' merciful shadow reached them and the sunset caught fire. A new guy was there, sitting in a folding chair beside a campfire he and Pastor Jack had built. Roy was old, though younger than Pastor Jack, grizzled and pink-peach in the golden hour, dressed vaguely military in cargo shorts, steel-toed boots latticed with abrasions, a vest loaded with pockets and patches, bucket hat. By way of greeting, he said, in a sand-blasted voice, "I brought cookies."

The four sat at awkward distances around the fire, ate mesquite-flour chocolate chip cookies, and talked. Roy croaked to Rose at length about mesquite flour, a superfood, and about his garden in Pahrump. He was apparently a retired park ranger, and indeed his cookies were marvelous.

Yellow Pine was a portent of things to come, Roy said, just one site of the green-energy gold rush: a sprawling blanket of industrial solar arrays, geothermal plants, and open-pit lithium mines in the works across the Mojave and the Great Basin.

Fran rattled off the arrays. "Just between here and Death Valley, it's Yellow Pine, Golden Current, Copper Rays, Sawtooth, Bonnie Claire, Chill Sun, Rough Hat, Titus Canyon, Busted Buttes One and Two, Gemini, Virgo, Sagittarius—"

Roy smirked. "Someone's an astrology buff."

"Cathedral Solar, Bonanza, Purple Sage, Jackpot." Fran snapped her fingers. "I'm missing some. Are you guys still hungry?" She fetched water-logged vegan hot dogs from a cooler. Pastor Jack went searching for sticks.

Green-energy gold rush. The governor said that. As when the president boasted of his plan to turn America's public lands into "an engine to fight climate change," one could observe, each time the man said it, how deeply it pleased him. Saying "green-energy gold rush"—meaning the energy industry murdering a massive swath of public land from the US-Mexico border to the Cascades—physically delighted the governor. His inflection was a rhetorical pat on the head for the striving twenty-year-old Yale intern who had so stylishly captured the state's stoke for turning America's spiritual outback into Silicon Valley's resource colony.

"I'm still hungover from the last gold rush!" Fran said. She'd grown up in Vegas, and longed for their home territory to get beyond boom and bust. The busts were brutal, increasingly close together, "and the booms don't hit like they used to." According to BLM's environmental impact statement, she said, after construction was done, Yellow Pine would provide zero to ten jobs. Likely the array would be operated remotely, from Florida.

Pastor Jack shook his head.

The array's lasting effect, Fran said—and Rose would confirm all this on the BLM website when she got home that night, staying up for hours devouring documents—was the "permanent loss or degradation of native vegetation" at the site. The forest in question was older than most cared to count. Yucca colonies grew for hundreds of years; creosote bushes spread in rhizomatic rings for thousands. Wasn't the oldest living creature on the planet a creosote ring? Rose offered.

"King Clone." Fran nodded, though she preferred the name Mother Crone. "In San Bernardino County."

"Creosotes at the Test Site survived the nuclear bombs," Pastor Jack said, checking his hot dog.

A skill that might soon come in handy, said Roy.

Wilderness deserved life, they agreed, and everyone needs wilderness to be whole, even people who never came out here. Especially them. Free, clean electricity for everyone was possible, had *been possible* for a while now, Fran said. "California could make PG and E pay for their sins and use that money to put solar panels on every other roof and over every other parking lot in the state!" Instead, the animatronic Ken doll governor repeatedly bent over for regulatory capture, his appointees on the California Public Utilities Commission steadily sabotaging rooftop solar. She said Nevada's state legislature could be the mavericks they wished they were and enforce a real sustainable energy revolution with a holistic land ethic.

Rose said, "You're playing my song."

But nope, Roy said: Both parties at every level of government were dead set on turning the ancient desert wilderness of the Southwest into the Texas oil fields of the twenty-first century. "They keep saying 'farm,'" Roy said. "'Solar farm.' I grew up on a farm in Iowa. Farms—I'm talking family farms, not factory farms—farms are *alive*. They're tended, cultivated, nourished. They nourish in return. Cycle of life. A solar array is scraped, sprayed with poison, dead as a damn doornail. So quit sayin' 'farm.' Don't piss on my head and tell me it's raining."

"And there's probably nothing we can do," Fran said.

"Next to nothing," Roy said.

Rose tried something from Al-Anon. "No situation is truly hopeless."

Fran pinched her wiener. "I like that."

"Hey, maybe you know this, Fran," said Pastor Jack. "Who was Charleston?"

"Like?" She pointed at the peak, the lights of Vegas glowing behind it.

Rose and Pastor Jack nodded.

"Wrong question," Roy said. "Not who. Where. Charleston, South Carolina."

"Some Southerners," Fran said, "miners, I think—named it during a rush."

"Hmm," said Rose. "Sort of disappointing."

"Pathetic, isn't it?" said Fran. "What's the mentality that comes out here and encounters a land unlike anything they've ever seen, land that God supposedly destined for you, and says, let's name it after"—Fran pretended to puke—"Charleston, South Carolina."

Roy shrugged. "Just homesick, I bet."

"We got a lotta Confederate names out here," Rose said. "The *Alabama* in Alabama Hills was a ship that sank. Longstreet was a general."

"I like the Indian names best," Pastor Jack said. "I like the Pahs: *Pah*rump, Ivan*pah*, Moa*pa*, Teco*pa*, No*pahs*. *Pah* means water, I'm sure you girls are aware." The girls were.

Distributing buns, Fran said it had been a bloody and failed experiment, the American West. So much slaughter in a quick couple hundred years! And the next few decades were looking to be even worse, especially in cities like Las Vegas, where soon it would be too hot for asphalt. No region of this malevolent nation, Fran said, sliding her blistered frank into a stale bun and pumping on a bottle of mustard she'd been crimping between her knees, should know the lie of the sacrifice zone more deeply, more intimately than the thirsty, smoky, forever-irradiated Southwest.

Rose sauced her dog and handed Pastor Jack the mustard. Fran seemed elsewhere, staring dismally into the fire. Without planning to, Rose asked, "Have you ever done therapy?"

Fran looked up. "Me? No. But I need to." She brought her hot dog to her mouth then halted. "I'm sorry, Pastor. Did you want to say a prayer?"

"That's okay," Jack said. "I been praying this whole time."

The Old Siren Trip

God, Rose loved Miles again. Every piece and part of him. Even the part of him that couldn't admit he loved her back. Especially that, since it told her he was free. She might have been worried, but from the moment Miles moved in, he'd been playing at getting her pregnant. Rose's role was to act like she didn't want it. Mostly she very much did. Too much, probably. It was not a game to her. Whenever she began to erect a little matchstick house of doubt inside her, it wasn't long before an earthquake of an orgasm flattened it. Their only conversation about contraception had gone like this:

Rose: I should probably let you know that I'm not on birth control.

Miles: This is fine.

Rose: I was on the hormonal stuff for, like, ten years and it was awful. Stunted my sex drive. Made me feel dead inside. Like an alien in my own body.

Miles: Hmmm. That's terrible.

Rose: I'm never doing it again. And I'm not really in a place in my life where I would have an abortion, if . . .

Miles: This is also fine.

END OF CONVERSATION.

So it was complicated, Rose reminded herself, muted in a meeting at her desk beneath the living room window, watching Miles disappear over the horizon on his trash-walk ritual, from which he'd return with new trash bags stuffed with old trash bags, with all manner of petrochemical discard: long-lost Mylar balloons, busted and brittle plastic flowerpots, shredded hoop-house tarps, disintegrating soil bags from the pot farms, countless red Solo cups, having high-graded the best finds and given them to Pastor Jack for his sculptures. Camera off, Rose waited for Miles to pick his way back to her. Every time afraid he wouldn't.

Whatever else he was doing—walking, reading, resting, noodling on his guitar, tinkering with the clothesline, organizing the recycling, tearing down dormant satellite dishes, ripping out defunct cable wires and flinging them into a pile by the shed—Miles watched the sky all day. He made them simple dinners, salad and vegetarian stews with fat slabs of buttered bread. Rose had him read *The Land of Little Rain* by Mary Austin, the Whitman of the West, and obsessed with her essay "Nurslings of the Sky," Miles began offering, while they ate, nightly cloud reports.

"Long, low parade of fleece blowing though all day, and a thin waffly contingent beyond that, very high up."

"Mostly clear today, then rippled lace hustling in from the east at rush hour."

"Lot going on out there today! Gauzy gravel rolling over Resting Springs, and a broody monsoon lollygagging over Fort Irwin."

Normalcy lurched toward them. The feds finally gave up enforcing the Borehole closure. Miles and Rose started soaking every day at sunset. Miles's unemployment was about to run out, the water table of his savings dropping precipitously. "Thinking bus driver," he said one day, fresh off a trash walk. "Pastor Jack says the school district has openings."

"Like Ed Abbey," Rose said.

"Like Ed Abbey," Miles allowed. "But hopefully, for your sake, a little bit better."

"A little bit better seems like a realistic goal. Ed Abbey didn't have Ed Abbey to learn from. The district's hiring drivers?"

"O yes," said Miles. "The old ones are dropping like flies."

Miles got the bus-driver job. Then came another loving shove from the universe. Rose received a call from HR inquiring about certain "incidents" involving Topher. In addition to pursuing young staffers romantically (which, okay), he'd apparently, during a bad reaction to a ketamine enema (he claimed) sent some untimely texts to a megadonor—dick pics and commentary on the topic of John Muir's alleged racism—and was presently on paid leave. Would, could Rose lead the team in his absence? HR wanted to know.

Certainly, she said, detailing her would-be response to the crisis: full transparency! She would personally reach out to the entire team and every major donor in the district to explain, if someone would first explain it to her, the seriousness of senior management's response to Topher's missteps (as HR called them) and the wider issues of equity and inclusion in Club leadership they exposed. Such a reckoning would be painful, Rose acknowledged, but it was the only path to true repair, no? And of course, were she elevated to management, Rose would fully support the staff's burbling efforts to unionize. Was not such solidarity the only way for the organization to—here she quoted a recent mandatory training video—meet the moment? "Now more than ever?"

That afternoon, Rose and the rest of Topher's team were invited to enjoy their own indefinite paid leave.

The county baths reopened! The Triangle reopened!

In the Kit Fox Café, a documentary about sharks played on the TV where in an ordinary café a menu might've been. Watching it from behind the counter was Travis, the baker with sad eyes and a long, granite-colored beard he wore in a braid. He asked Rose where she was from.

"Here."

Impressed, he asked Miles.

"All over."

Travis tugged his beard braid approvingly. "What brought you out here?"

Miles draped his long arm across Rose's shoulders. "A woman."

"That old siren trip," said Lalo one afternoon at the Rattler Room while Miles was at bus-driver school in Barstow.

"Exactly," said Rose. "I'm not a witch! I didn't lure him! I was minding my own business, and he shows up and starts overwatering."

Lalo either worked at the Rattler Room or was a very engaged regular. She was there every day, the steady right-hand woman of the flushed and frenzied brewmaster. She offered fresh rounds, delivered food from the café out to the patio, emptied ashtrays and disappeared dirty pint glasses and used napkin wads in a priestly sleight of hand. She brought Rose a bowl of vegan chili, opining it was Miles's pecker what brung him.

"You're absolutely right." Rose read Lalo "A Double Negative" by Lydia Davis:

"At a certain point in her life, she realizes it is not so much that she wants to have a child as that she does not want not to have a child, or not to have had a child."

"Except you already have one," Lalo pointed out. "But you maybe want another one?"

"Maybe." Certainly Rose had some niggling concerns about the timing, the hurtling velocity, the I-love-you thing. But since Miles had come back, she'd undeniably been wanting another baby. Or she never fully didn't want one. She definitely didn't not.

"Sometimes I don't know. Not up top, where knowing knows, you know?"

Lalo knew.

Mainly this risky sex made Rose very, very happy—a novel state of being for her. A little freaky, these uncharted depths of ecstasy. She tracked her menstrual cycle in giddy secret, creating in her journal a code of moon glyphs one might spot high up on canyon walls approaching a spring. When her ovulation window opened, Rose felt the breeze. She felt her egg release and—through the course of one bloaty, crampy, holy day—felt it implant. Nothing made Rose come like Miles a piston overhead and her below, inwardly willing the egg fertilized. Her word was *welcome*.

All the while, Miles officially liked her a lot. She wanted to give her love cleanly, rinsed of all transaction, condition, expectation. Love wasn't a debt, she knew, wasn't owed, wasn't on layaway. It did not have to be earned. Love could not be coerced through scarcity, cajoled by implied threats, should not be yanked back if unmatched like some sadistic philanthropist's so-called gift.

But Rose was thirty-nine-and-a-half years old, and while she violently rejected the common worldview in which her uterus was a ticking time bomb set to explode at forty, she did feel increasingly that there was someone waiting to be brought forth and she did feel strongly that they should be brought forth into love, not merely the feeling and the action but the word, risen from within and released on Miles's breath.

And she missed Juniper. There were no words for how she missed her and nothing to be done about it. She tried her mantra: June was safe, she was well cared for, et cetera, et cetera. Some days this helped; some days it didn't. Some days she could bear the separation; some days she couldn't. Some days longing curdled inside her. No breath could reach it.

It had occurred to Rose that maybe Juniper was the one she felt waiting to be brought forth, but Rose could not bring her any forther, legally.

Yellow Pine

Miles spent a week in Barstow for training. Resolving to pour her newfound solitude, pent-up mothering energy, and the windfall of free time made possible by Topher's randy shenanigans into collective action, Rose again went to Yellow Pine.

For a year and a half now, since Pastor Jack had introduced her to Fran shortly after the Trump administration "fast-tracked" the project, Rose had been sporadically supporting Camp Yellow Pine. She went to the seasonal campouts Fran threw, gatherings she called "poetry in motion," an exuberant mischief of artists, scientists, wonks, cranks, and hermits gathered against the array. Fran plugged a microphone into a solar-powered speaker. People sang, told stories, read poems, made speeches. Together they bore witness. When night fell they sat around a fire and filled each other's buckets, as June would say: broke bread, shared news, spitballed strategies, gossiped, joked, cried, and consoled. Mostly they talked shit about their despised elected officials.

Between the campouts, Rose came alone to relieve Fran. She would drive over from Tecopa, sleep a night or two in Fran's teardrop while Fran went to her girlfriend's in Nipton to shower, sleep in a bed, and reset her BLM clock so she wouldn't violate the agency's two-week backcountry camping limit. This way Camp Yellow Pine could continue uninterrupted without anyone getting ticketed or unintentionally arrested.

Rose pulled up to camp, found Fran basking naked as a lizard on a striped Mexican blanket in the afternoon sun, all shine and sinew, reading. Fran rose on her haunches and waved a parade wave, her face angular as agate, her smile wide, bright, and daring. Rose had a mild but long-standing crush on Fran, was mature enough to admit that another reason why she came to Yellow Pine. Rose enjoyed a number of erotic fantasies playing on heavy rotation whenever she came out, but she'd always been too intimidated to make a move. Against Fran's exuberant lesbianism, Rose felt like a bisexual phony. Plus Fran had the (mediocre) girlfriend, a major turnoff. So Rose had never felt the need for confession, courtship, or consummation with Fran. Just masturbating alone in her sheets was enough.

Today—objectively sexy as Fran was, reposed on her serape with Jean Baudrillard's *America*—Rose found her lust for Fran sun-faded against her brightly burning love for Miles. Kinda baffling, the fact that she could not see herself wanting anyone but Miles ever again. Bizarre actually, after half a decade of militant postdivorce solitude, like discovering a heliocentric model of her inner universe. Heresy, this faith, this devotion. It thrilled and terrified her.

Fran ditched Baudrillard and donned a kimono. The friends hugged. Shoving her feet into work boots, Fran asked, "What are you doing here?"

"It's time," Rose said, "two weeks."

"Wow, already?"

Fran rolled them a joint. Tall silver fence poles were up around the site, and between them stretched the tortoise exclusion fence, a tight, black, wire grid about two feet high. They walked along it for a while, smoking and riffing.

Yellow Pine was a construct, they reflected undergraduately, a fiction within a fiction within a fiction. Preceding Nevada's invention, the valley was the southwest edge of Deseret, Mormon country. Before that it was the northern frontier of Alta California, Mexico, and before that, New Spain. Before that and still it was Newe Sogobia, the unceded territory of the Nuwu, specifically the Chemehuevi and Pahrump bands, the latter unrecognized by the federal government. Yellow Pine was an invented place, invented to be owned, which until now it never had been, not in any real way. It had never had a fence around it. It had been open to anyone for camping, rock hounding, worship. Anyone could go out there for free, no questions asked. Yellow Pine, they decided, was a new nonplace invented to disappear the old true place. A curtain drawn across its sacrifice, like those veils of greenery logging companies leave alongside the highway to obscure their ghastly clear-cuts. Yellow Pine was a fake name for a real place that was really being killed for fake reasons.

They stopped where the fence line went through a family of yuccas, ground down into a void of mulch. Fran took pictures of it.

"And—not to be a poet about it," Fran said, "but as an image it's very interesting. And by interesting I mean revolting. A yellow pine would be a sick pine, a blighted pine. A deciduous pine, which doesn't exist. Something very wrong with it. Uncanny? The undead sublime."

"To me it sounds pretty," Rose admitted.

"O"—Fran grasped Rose's sleeve—"it's completely beautiful! It's like the feeling of a really warm day in winter, how intellectually you can know it's wrong, a bad sign, but the sun on your face still feels so good. The Germans probably have a word for that."

It hurt to think this way with Fran, and the hurt felt good. Or at least better than thinking alone. Was it this yellow pain, its wrong beauty, that brought Rose out here? Sometimes she didn't know why she came. Masochism? Rage? Grief? Acceptance? What should a person accept and not accept? What should she hate? (Mary Austin, in her final book, *Experiences Facing Death*, which Rose had written about in graduate school but did not at this moment consciously recall, said, assessing her life at its end, *No, I did not regret my hates—I have always hated lying and cowardice, and latterly I have spent a great deal of energy hating war.*) And what to *do* with hate? And what of love? What to do with that? Wasn't it love that pulled her out here? She hoped so. She felt the desert pavement fizz beneath her footsteps. Rose wanted to love on this land while she still could—a hospice sort of love. When Yellow Pine was gone, she wanted to be able to say she'd seen it. She wanted to be able to bear it, to be able to say what had been here. That this place mattered. Had mattered. Had lain relatively unmolested since time immemorial.

One hundred and thirty-nine adult desert tortoises. According to Fran's source inside BLM, that was how many tortoises the agency's biologist contractors had so far relocated to the dried-up spring across the road. "Refugees," Fran called them, borrowing the word of Ira, a cute, glum, nicotine-dependent Irish Jewish Marxist botanist who often camped with them. Death is a part of life. Rose knew that. Fran knew that. No sense hating it. The destruction at Yellow Pine was something else: early, preventable death. Avoidable sacrifice for excessive profit, the killability of the powerless, the shortsighted hacking up of an undulating old-growth forest that made the air they breathed.

Rose badly wanted the energy transition to happen—that desperate longing was part of what sent her out here. She was sick to death of the deny-and-delay tug-o'-war that had characterized so-called discourse her entire life, done arguing whether decarbonization should happen. She wanted to close that question, to proceed as though it *would* happen, as if the only question was how. One thing was clear: It couldn't happen like this. Once the contractors had dug up all the adult tortoises they could find, the chain link would unfurl across the poles, cutting off the land for good. Barbed wire would spiral atop the fence and full-blown construction would begin, crushing the baby tortoises, grinding them and every other living thing on and in Yellow Pine to dust. Until then, and *hypothetically*, Fran stressed, persons with Ira's and Roy's expertise could sneak into Yellow Pine at night, step over the tortoise exclusion fence, find the babies, and, before NextEra's goons arrived in the morning, rescue them. Of course that would be trespassing and, perversely, theft.

"Yes," Rose said. "Get the babies."

Fran's expression tautened severely. "Where's your phone?"

"In the car."

Fran patted her kimono for hers, found it in the deep well of a pocket. She tapped at it, opened up an encrypted app, scrolled, got distracted. Rose watched the sky until Fran remembered herself and handed her the phone with a video teed up.

Rose tapped play. It took a second to understand what she was seeing. A plastic storage bin with dirt at the bottom. Movement across the dirt. A zoom in. The baby tortoise stagger-swam toward a spear of lettuce, struggled to mount it, snapped a bite. "Attaboy" came Roy's unmistakable raspy voice from off-screen. The tortoise looked up, lettuce shred dangling from its beak, seemed to scowl. Then the video stopped.

"So cute," Rose said. "Send that to me."

Fran scoffed. "Can't, babe. You'll just have to have lived it."

"But I didn't live it."

There was more, Fran said. She swiped for Rose. In pictures the tortoise got bigger. A larger enclosure outside, shaded by paloverde and screwbean mesquite. A burrow in the enclosure made of hay and plywood loaded with earth. In a video, an unseen someone tapped a wand of measuring tape outside the burrow, and another young tortoise emerged, dust-coated and curmudgeonly. Rose swiped. Sunflowers and hollyhocks bobbed in the background of another video as three small tortoises circled the pen, their claws scraping against the rocks and railroad-tie walls, climbing on top of each other and tumbling off.

Rose swiped again. The next image was no longer in the garden enclosure. It looked down at the ground at some Yellow Pine–like place, framed around an adult tortoise shell. Empty, gold-brown patina on its plates. The shell had a huge hole in it, a gaping, jagged darkness, the plates peeled back as if it had been clawed open, which it had, Fran explained, by a badger. This was one of the adult tortoises relocated from Yellow Pine.

"A badger got one?" Rose asked.

Fran took the phone and frowned. "Got about thirty. According to my source."

Even in this grimness, Rose had to admit some wonder: She lived most of her childhood in this valley and did not even know it *had* badgers.

Fran looked tired when she left for Nipton, thinner. She shouldered her backpack, shook her small head, looked out at the place they'd soon lose, and said to it, "I'm sorry." Then she was off.

Wonder has its limits. Rose couldn't sleep that night, holding down Fran's teardrop fort against NextEra's array. She thought about how newcomers called this place empty, an effort (she chose to believe) to grasp its vastness, to get their heads around their own cosmic smallness. Here nothingness was a prayer, a worshipful cry let loose by the staggering expanse, obvious soul balm for city sprawl, as close as anyone could get to atonement for the monocropped former prairies of the Midwest, the South's drained and paved swamps, the raided forests of the East, the poisoned, burned, cow-chewed, bombed, plundered basins and ranges of the Mountain West, the panicked scrum of the moneyed throwing elbows on the storm-battered coasts. Places like Yellow Pine were the last swaths of intact wilderness on this fabulously abused landmass. The ground was the ground once walked by giant ground sloths! What could be more wondrous? Yet it seemed to matter not at all.

Rose wanted desperately to help. She wanted to get those babies. She rehearsed proposing the idea to Fran when she returned. Obviously she'd never be able to find a baby tortoise in the dark—that would be tough even for Ira and Roy. But couldn't she be a lookout? Help with supplies and transportation? Would they trust her enough to let her in? Did she trust herself to be let in? And if so, what then? This was not *The Monkey Wrench Gang*. This was the twenty-first-century surveillance state. Rose was not an arrestable, not with Juniper needing her. If anything came between them, there was no telling what Rose would do, whom she might betray. She couldn't put herself or her friends in that situation. She couldn't cross that line.

There is something in us that loves a line. Killable, not killable. Save, sacrifice. They were tempting concepts, mitigation, containment, all of the above. Destroy here, not here. War here, not here. But viewed from the teardrop, from against the tortoise exclusion fence, from a valley home to downwinders, this was plainly wrong thinking. That was not how destruction worked. Evil honored no line. It radiated everywhere. Embracing optional mass death to profit the same few who got us into this mess was self-harm at geologic scale. It was a deep, grievous injury to the collective soul. It hurt the place where we're all the same, and injury like that could never be contained. This loss could not be cordoned off. It flowed through us all, an oozing wound. When Fran came back the next morning, Rose confessed she feared this wound could never be healed.

"It can't," Fran said. "What's happening here happens to all of us forever."

"I wish I could help," Rose said impotently.

"You are."

Operation Plowshare

That day, back home at Nothingness Flats, Rose's period came, her uterus phasing unfazedly like the moon it was. Miles was back from Barstow for the weekend but far away. Emotionally, yes, but by evening he'd also moved down the road into the casita, which turned out to be owned by Pastor Jack. Rose couldn't blame him. Her secrets went beyond moon glyphs and despair. She was a narc. Harsh label, but one that was hard to shake, given the evidence.

Rose liked cannabis and small businesspeople as much as anyone, but the grow ops around Tecopa had pissed her off. The slapdash farms went up in an afternoon—ravenous entrepreneurs (cartel, some said) bulldozed an acre or five, threw up as many hoop houses as they could cram on the parcel, and dumped off an RV with some poor farmer living in it.

Pastor Jack had told Rose, when she first moved in, that the pot farms were run by "the worst people in the world." Maybe so, though it occurred to Rose that Pastor Jack's assessment might have been overinformed by fevered economic self-interest, as he himself was dabbling in clandestine horticulture at the edge of his acreage. Not to mention (it seemed safe to assume) bald fear of his new indigenous-looking, non-English-speaking neighbors. On the other hand, Rose had heard an upsetting number of gunshots coming from the farms.

After violence, her big worry was water. Where did they get it? Apparently enduring serious pillage, the Rattler Room turned off the free water spigot the hikers and nomads so loved. The water kiosk at the Triangle was cracked open regularly. Rose started having nightmares about industrial-grade pesticides seeping from the farms into the groundwater and leaching into the river.

Perhaps the Inyo County sheriff was not familiar with the concepts of rewilding or rematriation, which Rose had suggested as appropriate solutions for certain misdemeanor zoning violations in her email to narc@inyoco.gov. Instead, the cops busted all the unlicensed pot farms in Tecopa, which was all of them, including Pastor Jack's, slashing the shade structures and confiscating the plants. Then they sent Rose a postcard thanking her for her important contribution to Operation Plowshare. Pastor Jack brought the sheriff's postcard to Nothingness Flats that afternoon. It had ended up in his mailbox somehow, along with a five-hundred-dollar ticket.

Operation Plowshare. There was no telling if the sheriff knew the name was not original. If he knew, how deep was his knowing? Rose's guess was not too deep, that if anything he only dimly sensed a vague preexistence in the name's sturdy feel: Operation Plowshare. She'd never met the man but was familiar with the flyers he'd pinned to the bulletin board at the Triangle in some warped gesture toward community policing—DON'T SUPPORT PANHANDLERS!—with instructions to donate to a fundamentalist Christian charity instead. So it was possible that the sheriff did indeed intend to compare his deputies' plucking up cannabis plants and tossing them into a trailer while listening to classic rock to the United States exploding nuclear weapons on and in this very desert until 1992.

Pastor Jack handed the postcard to Miles. Miles read it and handed it to Rose. Both men stood and stared at her like they didn't know who she was.

Pastor Jack didn't know who she was, Rose knew, curled up on the couch later with cramps and guilt. In the handful of times they'd hung out, at the Shell station and at Yellow Pine, all he'd ever talked about was the Old West, Warren Buffett, and Jesus. He could keep his ignorant fucking opinions to himself.

But Miles knew her, Rose thought, watching him pack. (O, how fast he could pack!) Miles knew all about Rose of Sharon Williams, named by Jim Williams, her *Grapes of Wrath*–loving father, proud descendant of Okies and self-described pot martyr. Jim had been in jail in Hawai'i for most of Rose of Sharon's childhood, her earliest memory the raid. DEA helicopters whomping over the mango farm south of Kona, soon to be seized, forcing (Alice's word, its rationale opaque to Rose to this very day) her penniless mother to leave Jim and move six-year-old Rose of Sharon to Las Vegas, a place Alice and Jim had fled as teenagers. Rose remembered stepping off the plane at McCarran and feeling every drop of moisture sucked from her body.

First they'd stayed with Alice's brother on the west side, and what a shit show that had been. Truly: a two-bedroom tract house stuffed with six people and salted with the feces of various neglected pets—dogs, cats, rabbit, chinchilla, sugar glider. Next Alice and Rose of Sharon had fled from the pull-out couch in Vegas to the double-wide in Pahrump, where it was cheaper, where the animals shat outside. That was where, the new kid at the start of the second grade, patricidal Rose of Sharon insisted on being called Sharon. Miles knew about Sharon, knew Jim hadn't called the kid, not before he got out of jail and not after, had not *once* initiated contact with his daughter. Never visited her on the mainland, never sent a single present, letter, or card, though every time Alice made them talk, Jim claimed to have a whole cache of these just waiting on postage.

Rose got it, she understood. Who knew what a decade in prison did to you? Though Jim claimed to have had a ball inside, boasted about being a favorite of the lady warden, learning to play the harp, getting his GED, making the best friends of his life. Which had always sounded to Rose like a real haole take. Whatever, it was his shit, his guilt and shame and denial and whatever else her existence summoned to his surface. Rose wasn't carrying it for him anymore. He'd been dead since she was twenty-two and she was no longer giving the man free rent in her mind, except to despise him.

Miles had been at Jim's funeral. He'd met Alice there. (She'd loved him.) Miles knew Rose and Sharon. He knew who she was and where she came from. Where she came from was dirt. Who she was was shit.

It was for this reason, Rose knew, that Miles had packed up his van and moved into the casita. Little Sharon could not blame him.

Rose woke alone to the new wind and an empty fridge. Anger and abandonment ached in her gut. She drove to Pahrump for groceries, flipping off the casita as she passed it. Tourists in their experiencing-nature costumes milled about the Triangle. She flipped them off too.

The truth was she missed Miles, and fretted mightily about their future as she drove. He didn't want to break up, he'd said, just needed some space. But that made no sense when he'd been in Barstow all week and she'd been so alone at Yellow Pine. Who could need space with the Milky Way sprayed across the sky?

Yet, once caffeinated and provisioned, having survived another harrowing trip to Walmart, Rose also felt the casita setup working for her. Frida and Diego lived in separate houses. She liked the breathing room, looked forward to unobserved time, and considered it one of life's great joys to fart with impunity. She recalled Jane's three rules:

1. Focus on yourself.
2. Focus on yourself.
3. Focus on yourself.

So driving home, rather than obsess about Miles and their unknowable future, Rose decided to stop at the Triangle.

Consider the tourist. The unknown visitor blowing through. From the patio of the Rattler Room, Rose watched them amble and scramble, simultaneously anxious and oblivious, dust devils of compulsive documentation with zero presence. They staggered like adult babies across the highway to the WELCOME VISITORS! bulletin board wedged between the radiation-monitoring station and the post office. The bulletin board's chief aim was to protect the European body from the European imagination. It offered free park maps and weather reports in six languages, a urine color chart for monitoring hydration and other casual survivalist fundamentals to the French, Germans, and Dutch descending on the deadly desert.

Death was a palpable presence here. This, Rose offered unprompted to a pair of trim Dutchmen in spandex who arrived on e-bikes, was the place's medicine. Take its doomed mascots. Joshua Tree National Park shared with Sequoia, Redwood, Saguaro, and Glacier the ignominy of anticipating the local vanishing of its namesake: the Joshua trees of Joshua Tree were not expected to survive the century. There were other stands of Joshua trees throughout the Mojave, ancient groves in the Preserve, in Nevada and Arizona, and at the base of the

Eastern Sierras, each less protected than the last, each facing its own existential threat from capital, be it industrial solar, cattle, water banking, mining for lithium or—1850 all over again—gold. The Dutchmen showed little interest, but lit up at the word *gold*.

Lalo emerged from the bar and rolled a joint. She listened tenderly but without great concern to Rose's tourist rant. Appreciating the Mojave demanded a highly evolved environmental ethic best summarized as "don't call it a wasteland," Rose said. Each utterance of the word *empty* or *barren* made hard the malevolent swindlers who needed it so: mining, energy, peddlers of cheap, ugly, toxic housing developments and warehouse park exurbs, the defense-sector barons cashing in on the bases blasting the living land into oblivion, reducing this holy terrain to a grunt's punishment, only good for endless war. There could be, Rose proclaimed, "no right relationships on a ruined planet."

Lalo thought her friend was nuts. Maybe just heartbroken or too high. Weren't they having a perfectly right time on the patio on this entirely unruined day? She scribbled her roach into the gravel and dropped it into her breast pocket. "Your man still in Barstow?"

"He's back," Rose said. "Kinda."

Silently, knowingly (for Lalo had seen Miles's van at the casita that morning, as had the baker, as had the brewmaster) Lalo buttoned her breast pocket and resumed her sweep.

Rose tried to leaven her misanthropy in a way deserving of Miles. She thought fondly of the dropouts of Tecopa, the people she'd unthinkingly screwed with her self-righteousness. The freaks out here who'd heeded a wild call, fleeing soul death by getting up close to death death, its valley (however inappropriate that name, however unforgivably Anglo and afraid). Refugees of various systems, surveillances, and standardizations, her neighbors scoffed at the square world, murdered the normal, cunningly evaded creditors, ex-husbands, and

5G. A land of renunciates, visionary territory. She was a worldly worm compared to them, to the old heads and Natives who'd constituted the region's small but mighty movement for world peace. Still she liked thinking of herself among the people who'd stopped the bombs from raining down on—and later, burrowing into—that quadrant of Newe Sogobia the feds named the Nevada Test Site, people like Corbin Harney, the late spiritual leader of the Western Shoshone Nation, an antinuke activist who'd blessed the Borehole after Stamford Minerals gouged it into the edge of the wetlands, where five tons of gravel couldn't plug it. Rose had bought one of Harney's books at the Shoshone Museum, and after reading it dared to consider this place blessed.

Her mother had. Considered this place blessed. Alice had loved Tecopa, called its water magic. If ever they had the same days off, Alice and Chace would ride his Harley out here for "church," not Pastor Jack's but Corbin Harney's, Mary Austin's, Whitman's, Thoreau's. They'd take the waters, walk the clay hills looking for pretty rocks, get steaks and beer at Steaks and Beer. They'd always invite Rose, by then a churlish teen who hated her mother out of habit, with only the foggiest idea why. Alice had worked as a housekeeper on the Strip and then front desk at Longstreet in Amargosa Valley, forty miles away. Swing shifts, nights, she was gone a lot. But it was beyond that. Rose had been a bright, lively kid—spirited, in the euphemism of today's parenting literature—and this caused Alice endless problems. Not just the problems of money, of time, of distance, of who's supposed to drive you, of camp costs how much, tuition costs *how much*? Rose herself was the problem. Her wishes were punishment in waiting. Even between the more spectacular phases of Alice's unwellness, their precarity made Rose's avidity dangerous. Good news was a promise of looming doom. Rose had never accepted any of Alice's invitations to come out to Tecopa—a fact that hurt every day.

Alice couldn't do anything right. Rose felt stinging humiliation recalling her mom's be-okay rituals: dream catchers, crystals, sweat lodges, sage smudges. Men. Fresh off the plane from Hawai'i after leaving Jim, Alice had jumped into bed with every unhealed boob in Southern Nevada, culminating in Chace, King Boob. An unreliable, disappointing, profoundly immature person was the Christliest assessment Rose could manage. Chase was a big, jealous baby. And Alice was an addict, addicted to booze, to men, to work. Ceaseless, thankless, sickening, miserable, pulverizing work. Alice had been at work when June was born. She'd never even offered to take time off to come up to Reno for the delivery. Rose had not invited her. When Juniper was born, when Rose was calling out for her mother, Alice had been on the swing shift at Longstreet, just down the road from where the US government worked diligently in the name of science and security to irradiate them.

Operation Plowshare. Your tax dollars at work. Mine, Rose thought when the fighter jets rattled her windows. Maybe this was what her jackrabbit homestead book meant by "contested landscape." Contest, conquest, extraction, explosion. And against these, within them somehow: Peace. Solitude. Profound quiet. How still and subtle the place could be, as unassuming as its ancient and ungreedy plants. It was not a beginner's wilderness, though the sunsets, stars, and scale could grab even the most phone-addicted city slicker by the lapels. It was the sage's country, rewarding study and slowness, humility and mystery. The Mojave favored a mystic bent, like Miles's. One of the profound joys of Rose's life these days was watching him tunnel down into deepening stages of desert wisdom. The first stage, always, was fear. This was natural, the naturalness precisely what made it so frightening. The fear was animal. Modern man is not often in a place beyond GPS, rarely so aware that one wrong turn could kill him. To say nothing of the neo-Nazi flag Rose and June had yanked from the bullrushes near the Borehole and burned in their firepit that summer, or the Trump paraphernalia emporium in Pahrump still open for business to this very day.

Most people never made it out of the *Hills Have Eyes* stage, be they tourist or townie. Most people seemed so unable to accept death that they lashed out at the desert that reminded them of it, mistaking the land that kept them, that sustained their very being, from which rose the air they breathed and the water they drank, for an enemy combatant.

A well-documented effect of the Mojave Desert on the Western mind was expansion. Rose ached for Miles—so awake, so open, so seeking—burned to be beside him as he surrendered his mossy softness. She needed him to make her whole again, to reconstitute everything she'd cut into pieces inside herself. Seeing through Miles's eyes, she might unalienate herself, might stitch back together everyone she'd mistakenly made an individual. Together they'd welcome the return of those long thought lost. Here, a universe widely considered hostile or at best indifferent was revealed to be home. She wanted to be home, to be his home. Looking up at the Milky Way from Tecopa, you were right where you were meant to be—psilocybin optional.

Rose heard voices here. One night, not long before Miles came back (though she could not have known it then), she'd been up late at Nothingness Flats after putting June to bed. It had been a hard day between them—June was hot, sunburnt, bored, whiny, hated Tecopa. Why did her mom make them live in such a terrible place with no kids to play with, nowhere to go, nothing to do? Why did Rose have to live here? Why did she have to be so *weird?*

With June at last asleep, Rose tumbled deep into pain. It seemed suddenly that she had been very alone for a very long time. She thought, over and over again, *What the fuck am I doing with my life?* Dark-night-of-the-soul territory. Sitting at her desk, looking out across the moonlit dried-up sea, envisioning the bases bombing the valleys in every direction, clouds of poison dust rising from the proving grounds and construction sites, the rampaging industrial order sucking up water and scraping the land, Rose wanted her mom. She wanted to talk to Alice about all these shithead companies. She wanted to know what Alice would see from Nothingness Flats. She wanted help with June. She wanted to talk to her mother.

Grief-sick, pickled in impossible longing, wanting her dead, her mom, Jane. Even her pathetic dad would do. All Jane's gurus said the thing to do with pain was to let it connect you to everyone else. Rose tried to times her sorrow by seven million. As despair crested inside her, she heard a calm, clear voice.

The voice was not hers and not recognizable to her. It was not from her. It came from beyond.

This used to happen a lot when she was a kid—visits, voices, visions. Her Spidey-Sense, Alice had called it. Everyone was born with such gifts, was Alice's view, but few could tune in to them. Most who could, didn't. And the ones who did usually didn't talk about it.

The voice hadn't come to Rose in a long, long time.

It said, "Everyone is here now."

Rose heard—knew—felt—this to be a correction to an image she'd carried somewhere in her since Vacation Bible School (the only free summer camp in Pahrump), an image of God and the dead gathered above, looking down on her, watching, judging. In other words, the voice was against heaven. Instantly it cured Rose of her vertical arrangement of the world. It revealed this plane to be more than one big waiting room. If she had to name it, she would say it was the voice of the horizon.

Everyone is here now.

Rose felt the truth of this all through her. She was not alone and never could be. Everyone was here, now. "Wow," Rose said aloud to the voice. "Thank you."

"Thank you," she said again because once was not nearly enough. "Thank you. Thank y—"

And then her phone was ringing.

Miles. Her heart said that.

Then the phone said that.

"You're made vulnerable here," Miles said when Rose wished him to the Borehole at sunset. "That freaks a lot of people out."

"It freaks me out daily," she said.

He steeped himself down into the steaming, funky, cloudy water. "Even you?"

She nodded. *Me the most.*

"You can't deny fear," he said. "It comes from way inside."

"Maria's problem," Rose said, "in *Play It As It Lays,* is she's always *on* the desert. Never *in* it. Never *of* it. That's why she's so doomed."

"I need to go through it on my own," Miles said. "The fear." He glanced at Rose, wondering how this landed with her. She tried for steady. "That's what moving out is about," he continued. "Not the narcing thing—I mean, yes, ACAB or whatever, but I was gonna move to the casita before that. It's this"—he gestured out across the hot spring, the wetlands, the naked purple-blue mountains beyond—"all this. I know you love it. I know it's your place. But it's too much for me. I feel like a turtle without a shell, trying to live here. Trying again."

Rose nodded. Miles continued. "I mean, you can't even drink the water! I think I need a little space. Physically, psychically—I need room to be freaked out in peace."

"I get it," Rose said, genuinely getting it. "But the *Hills Have Eyes* stage is only the beginning. I think your fear is a sign."

"Of what?"

"Of the desert working its magic on you. The sun burning everything unnecessary away." She'd never told anyone about the voice of the horizon, but she told Miles now. "Everyone is *here now*," she finished.

"The dead too," Miles said.

"Especially the dead." The dead were the cement of her floors and the sand of her glass windows so often rattled by bombs. The dead were the bombs, and all bombs were were rocks pulled from the earth and hammered by industry into an evil shape. Even against this evil, inside it, despite it, her dead were here now, with her. They were at Yellow Pine. They *were* Yellow Pine. "This must be true everywhere," she said, "but I can only see it out here."

Miles nodded, that way he had of making her feel uncrazy.

"But I'm afraid," she said.

"Afraid of what?"

"That that's not a good enough reason to be here." To be away from Juniper, she did not say and did not need to say. Miles came toward her in the water. She let him hold her.

Held, Rose watched the sky show. Her vision was clear, a seeing without eyes, a hearing without ears. She was not away from Juniper. They were distant, but not separate. As unseparate as her ear against Miles's warm chest his good skin his beating heart its kissing valves saying without saying Everyone is here now.

Always Room for One More

The desert cooled into its second spring. The creosotes flowered and seeded again, the not-willows in the canyon drooped with lavender trumpets flecked with gold. New people milled about the Triangle—snowbirds, veterans, bikers, burners, drifters, drunks, hikers, rock hounds, cops, the lost. A neighbor Rose had never met expired in his sleep. Pastor Jack's son, Stu, was on the volunteer fire department and helped carry the body out of the trailer. "So many guns in there," he told Rose at the Rattler Room.

The bromie in Rose's bedroom bit it. The fig too. Miles was depressed, he confessed over the heart of Jesus rotted in its pot. Had he been working his prongs? He'd not. Come to think of it, she'd never once seen him phone a single friend.

Living apart was not the problem, they agreed. Miles had a sweet setup at the casita, and they had lots of sleepovers. The sex was better than ever—intense and undulating, loads of eye contact and laughter, Miles coming inside Rose with intention. But afterward he got tetchy, hard on himself. He spun out into slogans and koans. They put their phones, laptops, and June's iPad in an old microwave Rose kept out by the shed for this purpose and discussed.

They dreamed of a time after America. Right side of history, they said—rotted empire—become ungovernable—spiritual obligation—there are babies and there is bathwater—spray paint budget—arrestables—certain privileges everyone should enjoy—hundreds of sovereign peoples within this garbage nation—within beneath above beyond after again—imagination freer than any state.

"I love you," Rose said without saying, heard without hearing, insomnious in bed beside Miles when he finally fell asleep. She listened to him breathe, to his being breathed—transformation without effort. She tried to match her breath to his, tried to receive the snake plants' off-gassed oxygen. But her chest was tight, had no room, and she struggled to accept their offering. Why for her was simple inspiration—a supposedly automatic process!—such a tussle?

She got out of bed, took the bromie outside, the naked fig, dumped them from their pots off the edge of the deck. She held a short, silent funeral for them in the moonless dark. *Goodbye,* she eulogized wordlessly. *I'm sorry.*

As she turned to go inside, the coyotes began to sing. Always there was one who didn't even try to harmonize. *The only,* Miles had called him once their first time around. He was his own. Just completely audaciously an only. Another question Rose had lately was to what extent do we ever do anything again. Is time a line or a circle or something else? She listened to the only yodel while the rest of his family sang.

"The only," she said when Miles emerged sleepily onto the deck.

"What?" he said. Then, "It's a spiral, I think. That's what everybody's saying. A line that's a circle that makes a spiral. The seasons, the days. Like a record spinning. And sometimes a new track gets so close to the old track you overhear it. Sometimes they overlap, play at the same time. Sometimes they get stuck."

Rose nodded. Miles held her from behind, a sleeping bag for her soul.

"Or you *see* it," he went on in her ear. "Sometimes the past comes back around so close you can see it."

"Like a comet."

"Or the Milky Way." He pointed. There was no moon, and they could see it, the first coyote's breast milk spray, the open arm of their own galaxy. It made Rose dizzy.

"Like I can't get my bearings."

Miles said, "I know right where you are."

"Where am I?"

"You're on this side of the portal."

"I'm here," Rose tried.

"I'm here too," he said. "You have to trust me. I told you that from the beginning."

"I know."

"I'm not him."

"I know."

"I'm new."

"No, I know."

Later, legs aloft, Miles the lovingest piston overhead, Rose knew. She made room in her for the knowing and relaxed into the room. She draped her inner walls with a honeyed blanket of welcome for Miles, for their future being within, the cell ball, the cytoplast if you prefer. Silently she spoke to the new one. *We are ready for you.*

We meaning her and Miles and Juniper? Rose revised her reverse clairaudience.

I am ready for you. There's always room for one more.

They would address the delicacies of blended families and planetary resources another time. (Probably the new one already knew.)

Some Cassandras

Rose would freely admit—were there anyone around to admit it to—that she was cranky, PMSing, overcaffeinated and weak of spirit when she allowed herself to become vexed by *The New York Times*. IS THIS THE YEAR YOU FINALLY READ A BOOK ABOUT CLIMATE CHANGE? the paper wanted to know. Miles had left for training in Barstow before dawn, and all morning Rose stewed, though truthfully the article in question was a harmless trumpeting of some solid primers worth reading. Still, she got stuck on the headline. She fixated on it, obsessed with this You. *Who are "You"?* she wondered bitterly through the first half of a blustery but otherwise beautiful day. And why start now?

Certainly not to inform Yourself, she thought. You don't need to Finally Read a Book about Climate Change to get the bad news. For that we have—better late than never—these newspaper articles You're so fond of. You get it. Your kid definitely gets it, probably picked it up from every other movie and show. "We're trashing the earth." Juniper said that.

Needing a change of scenery, Rose put her favorite Books about Climate Change into her backpack with her towel and biked to the

Borehole, only to find it overrun by hot young bozos from Vegas making content and blaring EDM from a waterproof wireless speaker. Seething, Rose bailed on the Borehole and, though it was barely noon, pedaled down to the Triangle and posted up at the Rattler Room to read and get drunk in community, thinking how despite decades of fantastically profitable delay enabled by fantastically expensive propaganda resulting in an entire generation of collective repression and misplaced anger, the basic gist of Climate Change could today be grasped by any sleepwalking dodo with a subscription to Disney+.

O yes, You get it. The broad strokes at least. Enough to know You don't want to know more. Because hey, You're not perfect! You're no saint! If You knew more, You'd have to *do* more. You'd have to get your own house in order.

To that Rose would say, Nah!

In this case, she argued to the preoccupied brewmaster on his belly below the bar where he wrestled with a clogged tap line, weren't the politics of personal responsibility plainly the bunk stalling tactics of the status quo? The everybody-do-your-part logic made it conveniently hypocritical for anyone with a carbon footprint—a concept invented by the oilmen!—to express even the mildest quibble with a regime of rampant, ongoing ecocide. Today the everybody-do-your-part garbage she had been obliged to include in every Club appeal rang laughably hollow, a tragically effective engine of distraction, exhaustion, and disempowerment.

Rose had changed her habits, was a vegetarian, bought less, used less, thought more about what she did buy and use. She thrifted, biked, drove a hybrid, walked when she could. That was a nice way to live. Kicking compulsive consumption was one of the most rewarding maneuvers of her life in fact. But it was a far cry from absolution. From regarding one's own existence as morally neutral, let alone a gift, let alone oneself the walking embodiment of God-consciousness

(Jane's philosophy). The more Rose lived intimately with her own alleged destructiveness, the more she countenanced the supposed wrongness of the very best thing she'd done with her life—making Juniper—the more she learned about the activities of the American Petroleum Institute and their ilk, the more she had come to think "everybody, do your part" was short for "everybody, do your part and do it perfectly, purely, all the time somehow from within a petrochemical economy designed to make that impossible, or else shut the fuck up."

Lo, Rose saw that the recycle-reduce-reuse refrain she had imbibed and regurgitated all over her loved ones handily relocated the responsibility of right living from the architects and profiteers of climate collapse to the individuals suffering under it. She'd seen it day in and day out at the Club before being rescued by this heaven-sent paid leave: staff, volunteers, donors—they'd all swallowed hook, line, and sinker the false gospel of overresponsibility, their outrage eddying in their own impeccable recycling bins, their glass jars of whole grains, their bamboo toothbrushes and writhing compost piles, when it ought to have flowed up. And though they all dressed like they'd stepped out of the Patagonia catalog, hardly any of them even went outside! They'd all—and Rose had to include herself in this—become self-righteous harpies, strutting from their standing desks to the break room and back with their correct reusable water bottles spattered with faded stickers demanding radical solutions that would never come. Desperately they badgered everyone around them about the massive impact of their every choice, policing their friends and neighbors, methodically alienating positively everyone with any shred of sympathy for their cause. "It's a trap!" Rose shrieked at the unmanned bar. "Rex Tillerson's favorite wet dream! Don't You fall for it!"

The brewmaster snorted and rose from under the bar, a yeasty spatter across his spectacles. "Two words," he said. "Cloud seeding."

Just the sort of technocratic delusion that would've spun her out. But Rose was rested. She was done with guilt. Done with morality plays and misdirected rage. She toasted to cloud seeding with the brewmaster and went to the Kit Fox for coffee cake. There she found Travis rapt by his shark documentary, eyes swampy, worrying the tassel of his beard braid. Really the shark documentary was a whaling documentary, Travis explained, for it was made in the seventies and to get the footage of so many never-before-seen shark behaviors the filmmakers had tailed a Japanese whaler. The whaling was largely offstage, Travis said, but here came the unintentional climax: a conveyor belt delivering bloated whale carcasses up onto the whaler like forgotten luggage. Waterfalls of blood cascading into the sea, the grisly occasion for the film's thrashing carnival of sharks.

Rose couldn't. She went outside. She seethed for the fog of universal culpability to burn off before it drove anyone who cared about the living planet permanently insane. Despite the rhetoric that had been required in her fundraising pleas—even now they were automatically zapped up to space and pinged down unwantedly into how many thousands of innocent inboxes—Rose would not attribute the extinction agenda to the whole of humanity, because they were not all equally responsible. *Capitalism,* Ashley Dawson wrote in *Extinction: A Radical History* (a book decidedly not on the *Times'* list for You, which Rose reread on the patio, secretly hoping to intercept Miles after training), *has unleashed waves of enclosure, imperialism, warfare, and ecocide over the last five hundred years that have benefitted a very small segment of humanity while displacing, immiserating, enslaving, and destroying countless numbers of people, animals, and plants. Everyone is not equally responsible for the destruction of nature.*

Lalo peeked at the cover of *Extinction* on one of her sweeps. "Cheery."

"It *is* cheery," Rose called weakly after her. "Ashley and I absolve You!"

But Lalo was gone. The beat goes on, thought Rose, that tiresome binary toggle between hope/despair, hope/despair, a paralyzing feedback loop obscuring a most uncomfortable question: What have You done to deserve hope? *Lordy,* she thought, her head swimmy in the late-day sun, *You want an awful lot from Your end-time prophets.*

People always said, when they learned what Rose did for work, that's *good.* But work was not good; work precluded good. Work was the problem. Or the problem was that everyone getting paid to solve the problem was at work. And the actual task before them was not to fix it. The task before them was work. Make content. Raise money. Hit your numbers. Grow the database. Stay on message. Manage the brand. Dangle endorsements. Win elections. Impress the boss. Pay your student loans. Don't get fired. Everyone with any sway was working. No one wanted to hear from her sad stack of books.

Rose had a fantasy going, had had it going for a while now, that all this would get unstuck if everyone would get out on the land. Just walk this drastic place bristling with omens. Secretly she thought this desert more adept than any writer or activist ever would be at laying bare settler madness. Its ghost towns and zombie subdivisions were anti-capitalist manifestos written in concrete. Doomsteads, trash art, war games scarring, bushes that survived nuclear blasts. Rose needed Books about Climate Change to do to her what this place did to her, the written equivalent of gaping up slack-jawed at more stars than you knew there were, a book that read like trying to breathe in record heat, a map of how we got here, with the exits clearly marked.

An oft-observed characteristic of desert thinking was uncommon clarity, the same unobstructed view that summoned to these parts astronomers and geologists. How sharp things became out here, where one could read the mountains and the mines where mountains used to be. "Climate collapse is an outgrowth of the atomic age," Rose beseeched Lalo when her friend was foolish enough to emerge for a cigarette within earshot. "Which we should not misunderstand as a bygone era or a style, not some retro mid-century aesthetic deployed by Pixar, but an ongoing regime of normalized global mass death at the hands of industry and its bought-off government."

Lalo grunted in affirmation. She despised the government.

"We act like these things ended, the atomic age, the Cold War. We periodize them, compartmentalize them. Old people say, 'This is like 1968, this is like the Cold War,' like they have their war and we have ours, when actually we have theirs *and* ours. The carnage is accruing. The atomic age never ended! We have not disarmed. And if they can do it to the desert, they can do it anywhere. The desert, according to the United States, is skull and crossbones all the way down. And that's how it's been when we've had plenty!"

Lalo puffed on her rollie around an expression that Rose took to mean *when you've had plenty*. Fair enough.

"The whole setup," Rose continued, "has been stingy, cruel, wasteful in times of—artificial! unevenly distributed!—abundance. And abundance is not what's coming. You don't have to be a wandering desert father to see the wealth gap widening until the point-one percent enjoy unlimited screen time in their New Zealand fortresses and the rest of us are dead. Ever heard of China Lake?"

Lalo had (her ex-husband was military) yet Rose expounded.

"Dry lake bed on the other side of those mountains. Became a bombing range when a couple of Caltech professors got into a little prop plane, flew over it, looked down, said, 'Yep.'"

Lalo concurred that there was some secret shit going down at China Lake, and not just the bombs and drones. "Talking remote viewing. Extraterrestrial technology. Crash recovery. CIA shit. Black ops."

"Exactly," Rose said, with only the vaguest inkling what her friend was talking about. She went on enumerating her objections to the heroic tradition. "Messianic thinkers like end-of-the-world stories because they make us feel important. As scary as the end times are, it's less scary than the simple fact that the world will probably spin on without us. Most of us would rather be incinerated in a nuclear fireball than become plain old worm food."

Lalo rolled a fresh cigarette, tucked it behind her ear, and rolled another for Rose. Rose lit it, said thanks, then dove headlong into a lecture about the attention economy, how butchery got whipped into money on social media, man's inhumanity to man rammed through the smart phone and monetized, all of us downgraded. "That's not my word, that's what they call it: human downgrading."

"Who's they?" asked Lalo, taking a drag.

"The boys who made it. Their professors at Stanford, at MIT. They made this unethical, manipulative device to hijack our simple primate nervous system. The phone—"

"And really we shouldn't call it a phone," Lalo said, plucking a fleck of tobacco from the tip of her tongue. "It's a tracking device."

"A self-inflicted Harrison Bergeron," said Rose, the reference lost on Lalo. "Kurt Vonnegut? Whatever. My point is, it feels good no matter what news it brings. I'm talking chemically. In your brain. The thing bleeps and you get that tingle. That little red dot releases a mist of pleasure chemicals, an artificial orgasm, jackpot at the feelings casino. So, like, on some subconscious synaptic level, it *feels good* to get a picture of the last rhino, or a four-year-old refugee washed up dead on a beach. We get off on it."

Lalo looked at her phone. Flipped it face down on the table.

Rose soldiered on. "It also feels *really* bad. Have you ever noticed that? Like something is happening *to* you. Like you are being done to. Which you are. Which makes it that much easier to accept the rising tide of fascism. We're getting a lot of practice at having zero agency, picking up the phone looking to do *X* or *Y* and emerging from a fucking mine some lost amount of time later, having done none of what we wanted and a lot of stuff we didn't want and not knowing why. How can we get it up to be troubled by the jalopy of our democracy when for so long now we have been so unequivocally unfree?"

Lalo shrugged. "I like the podcasts." She flipped her phone over and pecked at it awhile. When she returned, she said, "But I sure do lose a lot of time in there."

Rose clawed another book from her backpack, *Desert Notebooks* by Ben Ehrenreich, also not on Your list. "*Time is not an independent vector that pushes on,*" she read to Lalo, "*stubborn and cocksure, taking us to a place called the future. It lives in our bodies and in the stars, in the mountains that rise up from the sea floors, in the wind and rain that wash the mountains back into the sea.*"

Lalo moaned. "I know that's right."

"Guy lists an insane number of clocks in this book," Rose said. "My favorite is the ancient Chinese incense clock. It changes smell depending on how long it's been burning."

"Dope," said Lalo.

"*Time is motion,*" Rose read. "*It favors circles, spirals, and ellipses, but it also does not mind explosions.* Here, listen to this: *Trauma stops time.* He's talking about being a reporter in failed states. *Catastrophe breaks all cycles.*"

"You've read all these?" Lalo regarded Rose's stack of books as though it were a Superfund site.

"Not, like, today," said Rose.

"And you're just riding them around on your back I guess," Lalo said with pity. Then, "There's lotsa better ways to run things than on gas."

"Yes!" Rose brayed. "Community solar in the built environment! Free clean energy for all!"

"Or," said Lalo, "that shit the aliens is onto."

Just then, Miles's van rounded the hill. Rolling toward the Triangle, it popped gravel and slowed to a stop beside the Giving Rock. Rose watched Miles lope across the road, watched his face light up when he saw her bike. He found them on the patio, said, "Hey, Lalo," and kissed Rose in the crook of her neck.

"How was Barstow?" she asked.

Miles stuck his tongue out and panted. "Barstow is a hard town."

He got himself a beer and settled in to read a Bible-looking book with gold letters stamped on its cover. *A Course in Miracles.*

"Now *that's* a great book," said Lalo before heading back into the bar.

Rose had never heard of it.

"Marianne calls it the *Ulysses* of self-help," Miles said. Later, he looked up from the book and said, "I'm thinking of talking to my dad again."

"No time like the present," Rose said, flipping through another book from her stack: *Ill Nature*, 2001. "*Time is repetition, a circle,*" she read. "*This is obvious. Day and night, the seasons, tell us this. Even so, we don't believe it.* Joy Williams said that."

"Maybe people believe it now," Miles said. "Maybe people feel how wrong it is to mine a mountain now that we're the mountain."

Maybe, Rose forced herself to think. Maybe You believe it. Maybe You heard the crack when time broke, a snap-rip at the exact moment when grief overwhelmed productivity, proving it an absurd and cruel way to measure a life. Maybe the very shape of time has shifted beneath You as it has Rose, when after another slide of the sun across the sky without June beside her, without Jane beside her, without her mother, without Miles, she retired to her hammock to watch the stars come out, to cry until her ducts ran dry, then light her own version of an ancient Chinese incense clock. This time's not going to smoke itself.

If You have been there, aswirl in time's burning eddy, watching, thinking, You have questions. Why were the children on strike? What did Greta mean when she said, *I want you to panic. I want you to feel the fear I feel every day?* You are curious: How exactly does one feel another's fear?

Easy. You absorb it.

Back when she attended such things, Rose noticed three inevitable moments come Q&A time at the doomer discussion panels she organized for the Club. First, the frantic and entitled demand for Hope™. Second, the question of whether one (or, more often, one's adult children) should have a child. And third, yoked tightly to the second, the thing Rose kept thinking of, the moment that was really stuck in her craw, always, always, always: population control.

At first blush it seemed a totally relevant question in any conversation about sustainability and overshoot. Carrying capacity and carbon footprints had featured prominently in her college environmental-science classes. Yet the more Rose thought about it now, on the back side of the flattened curve, the more she found population control being so close at hand in the collective psyche pretty darn troubling. It was like the weird wrong mole marking the ecofascist tumor that had been metastasizing in the toxic sludge of "the climate debate" for Rose's entire life. For forty years we allowed ourselves to be lied to, paid executives record profits to take years off our lives. This had serious and largely unacknowledged costs. Helplessness and dread festered within us, collectively and individually. The deniers especially. But Rose was not talking to Them now. She was talking to You.

You daren't Read a Book about Climate Change. You stuff the truth down. You glimpse it only out of the corner of Your eye, where decisions blur into inevitabilities, where policy failures become laws of nature. You let Your rich grandpas plunder the commons rather than make them put a bunch of solar panels on their parking lots. As far as Rose could tell, the solution You seem to have settled on was three-pronged: recycle, don't have kids, and force sterilize the Southern Hemisphere. In other words: Be rich or kill Yourself.

"People have been predicting the end since the beginning," Miles said, having brought another round—beer for him, water for Rose—and examining the Ehrenreich. "Especially after industrialization, especially again with the rise of modernity. People went berserk at the bicycle. The Qing dynasty nearly crumbled when the emperor got a landline. People have been Cassandra-ing civilization since we've had civilization."

To which Rose was obliged to screech, "*Cassandra was right!*"

Miles smiled patiently. Rose hated herself for making him be so patient. He said, "I'm merely observing that you tend to apply an apocalyptic rubric to your life."

"Apocalyptic as in *apocalypsis?*" Rose said. "Unhiding? Unveiling? Hell yes, I do. I don't think it's at all insane—"

"I didn't say insane—"

"—I don't think it's *insane* to ask Yourself at regular intervals who do You want to be in community with when You get killed for gasoline? Is what You are doing right now what You want to be doing when You die?"

Miles's eyebrows arched skyward. "Is it?"

"Lately, yes." She'd met a bone-deep calm walking the canyon, soaking in the Borehole, being beside Miles. She met it out at Yellow Pine. Like a terminal diagnosis met with a shrug and a smile. *All this was temporary anyway.* "It's not that I'm not afraid," she said. "I'm afraid all the time." Sometimes she measured time in tears, noting the hour she was out. "But I don't feel especially confused."

How long had she been this way? Probably since her and Miles the first time around. He brought it all back again. And somehow made everything new.

"Can I read you something?" Miles said, lifting his woo-woo Bible. Rose said he could. "*The end of the world,*" he read, "*is not its destruction but its translation into Heaven.*"

What she was most afraid of was not the end of the world but losing him again.

GIV HVN

The next weekend, Fran threw a campout at Yellow Pine, and Rose brought Miles. Stopped at the Smith's in Pahrump for beer and grillable veg, he asked to see the house she grew up in. "Can we see the burro dunes?"

"Another time," Rose told him. "I can only take so much psychic bloodshed in a day."

In fact she was in a grand mood, eager to show off Miles to her friends and to introduce him to Yellow Pine. What was left of it. Together, they would face it. She felt like she could do anything with him next to her, felt such peace with him in arm's reach that when they pulled up to the site and Miles parked on the side of Old Spanish Trail behind the Chinook and said, "Give heaven," Rose gave it, gestured to Yellow Pine with a flourish, and said, "It's yours."

Miles turned off the van and pointed to the Chinook's license plate: GIV HVN.

A respectable turnout, they observed. Looked to be about forty people. Rose recognized most of them: Pahrump locals from the Facebook group, Fran's grad-student buddies and her professors from UNLV, old heads retired from the school district, the Park Service, the Test Site. Pastor Jack, piling paper plates on a folding table, nodded but kept his distance.

The chain-link fence was up around Yellow Pine, barbed wire spiraled across the top. The transmission tower and battery banks were built. Floodlights had been erected, and a booth now stood at the entrance to the array, a security guard's rent-a-cop go-kart parked in front. Rose led Miles to the fence.

"NextEra promised to 'mow' the vegetation," she told him. "That was the so-called solution they came up with when we made a stink. But as you can see—" The site had been denuded, bulldozed, and sprayed. The land was scraped, its washes filled with gravel. Though there was no wind elsewhere in the valley, dust devils of alkali poof dirt spiraled up from the site on columns of heat. About half the panels were installed, shimmering in the sun like the water they weren't.

Rose clung to the chain link, self-consciously trying to take a moment for everything lost. She noted for Miles the segments of black pipe half buried intermittently along the fence, meant to shade the refugee tortoises as they circumnavigated the array, starving to death. Mitigation.

Ira greeted Rose at camp. Ira was probably the bravest person Rose knew. Dashing, neurotic, crusty, and deranged, this tattoo-scrawled, prep-schooled son of an oil lobbyist and the most high-powered lawyer in Las Vegas after Oscar Goodman. Ira had forsaken his parents' plunder, first implicitly by studying philosophy and labor at SF State when he'd been legacy at UChicago, then explicitly when, after disappearing into the Bay Area anarchist scene for ten years, he emerged like a tortoise from brumation to unceremoniously inform his parents that he'd give any inheritance they left him, down to the last dime, to their most loathed political enemies.

"Ira went to Syria," Fran had once whispered to Rose in the awestruck tone reserved for combat veterans. It was unclear to Rose what this meant. She did not know what all exactly was going down in Syria, had meant to look it up.

Rose gave Ira a squeeze. He smelled smoky, grief-ripe. Noticing Miles, Ira immediately set about preempting the charge of NIMBY-ism that so drove him nuts.

"We need renewable energy infrastructure," he explained while helping them unload the van. "We're probably gonna need *some* industrial solar," he told Miles as the two shuffled a cooler over to the folding tables, "but we need to build it on purpose."

"*Justly,*" Rose said like a grade-grubber.

"Is Bechtel the one to do that?" Ira asked.

The men set the cooler in the dirt. Miles fished out a Tecate, snapped it open, offered one to Ira and one to Rose. "Bechdel," he said. "Like, Alison? The cartoonist?"

"Bech*tel*," said Ira, cracking open his beer.

"Defense contractor," Rose helped. "They built the Hoover Dam, bunch of pipelines, bunch of nuclear shit. . . ."

"Privatized the Lawrence Livermore lab," offered Ira, "did the Big Dig."

"Hanford," Rose said. "Ivanpah."

"Kuwait!" cried Ira. "Stole Bolivia's water. The fucking wars in Iraq! Mistakes were made, man." Transitioning off fossil fuels would take a new land ethic informed by indigenous wisdom and the latest scientific knowledge, he said. "An understanding that the desert is keeping us *alive*, not a wasteland waiting to be ransacked." Ira said what people misunderstood, and corporations pretended to misunderstand, as a frightening expanse of nothingness (dirt and weeds at best) was shockingly alive. This life needed constant reiteration.

"Tortoises," Rose said, "badgers, kit foxes, deer, bighorn sheep, mountain lions, wild horses!"

Ira scowled. "You're not a wild-horse person, are you?"

"You're not?"

"I don't cosign the ungulates," he said. "The ungulates I do not fuck with."

Miles said, "Aren't wild horses the majestic symbol of the American West?"

"Burros built this place," Rose murmured.

"Majestic," Ira winced, "not so much. But a symbol of the American West *for sure*. Accidentally accurate. An invasive European war machine trampling springs, shitting everywhere, fucking nonstop, taking more than their fair share."

"They're animals," Miles said, "doing what animals do."

"There was a community here, is my point," Rose said. "A community of divine beings most of us will never see."

"Don't deserve to see," said Ira.

Miles frowned. They stood quiet for a while, until Fran emerged from her teardrop, finished tutoring online on her solar-powered computer. Rose hugged her and introduced Miles.

"What's this?" Miles asked Fran about a man-high cone of rocks piled near the Yellow Pine fence.

"That's our mizpah," she told him.

"Some biblical shit," Rose said.

"A mizpah," Fran said, "marks a boundary. When Jacob, I think it was, left his father-in-law's house with his wives, eventually they met up, the two men—"

"After, like, a *lot* of attempted murder," said Ira.

Fran nodded eagerly. "The father-in-law, I forget his name. He was like, 'Okay, I get it: My girls are grown now, they make their own decisions. They want a new life with you, Jacob. But you have to promise to be good to them. If you do, I won't try to kill you anymore. I won't cross into your territory. And you don't cross into mine. Deal?'

And Jacob was like, 'Deal!' And they built a mizpah there, at the boundary."

"Like a 'you shall not pass' kinda thing," Rose said.

"A watchtower," said Fran. "Because God is watching. I forgot to say that. It's like, God has witnessed our agreement."

"But they"—Miles thumbed behind him at the array—"Bechdel? NextEra. They haven't agreed to anything."

"Right," said Fran, smiling like she knew something they didn't. "So it's a little different that way."

"It marks death," said Ira. "In Jewish tradition. You see them all over the desert, wherever someone has died. Car accidents usually. A lot of time people add crosses."

"Like a cairn," Rose said.

Miles turned from the mizpah, taking in the open and purpling valley. He said he'd love to see a tortoise or a bighorn. "We don't have them in my mountains."

"We barely have them anymore in ours," said Ira. "If it's encounters with charismatic fauna you're after, you were probably born at the wrong time."

"Although!" Fran broke in. "I saw a kit fox at camp last week! You hungry?" Without answer, she joined some others making food.

Meanwhile, Joskie returned from his ablution at the far edge of Yellow Pine where, he informed them, a huge yucca family he'd known had been mulched. He and Rose hugged for a long time. Joskie turned to Miles, said, "Hey, guy," and hugged him too.

Joed, a.k.a. Joskie, was a world-class hugger, a jolly sandalwood-smelling fellow who came out to Yellow Pine from Vegas, where he was a professional clown, freelance graphic designer, and Yoruba initiate. His father was a locally famous lounge singer, a protégé of Sammy Davis Jr., and his mother the matriarch of a freed-slave ranching dynasty in Oklahoma. Joskie had four adorable kids brought forth by three different mothers, and he was still in a relationship with each woman. "It's complicated," he'd told Rose when she met his kids at a campout. "Then again, it's not: We all love each other."

"Is that how it's done in the Yoruba tradition?" Rose had asked.

"Girl, no," Joskie'd said, rolling his golden-brown eyes. "That's how it's done in the Bay Area."

Joskie turned to Miles. "So!" They were all excited about the new guy and coming on strong. "I'm for sure not one to go all in on the scientific worldview—actually I think it's"—he did the robot and a robot voice—"pretty evil." Ira jeered, smiled, and Joskie went on.

"But we have learned *a lot* about desert ecology since the first industrial solar was built out here, like, a decade ago? Scientists who bother to know know that, just like tree forests are interconnected, the desert is also, like, latticed"—he threaded his fingers—"with a network of roots, microbes, lichen, and fungi. This network feeds on dead stuff, minerals, sunlight."

"And moonlight!" called Fran from where she cooked.

"You heard about that lady who discovered that forests talk, cooperate, *care* for each other?" Joskie said.

"A lady *scientist*," Ira said.

"Same deal out here." Joskie gestured to the array. "The cryptobiotic crust, it's called, that connects it all, was *spectacular*. Massive black splotches on the desert that turned blue and green whenever it rained, feeding everything, bringing the desert back to life."

"That's where they got the idea for the resurrection," Rose said, presenting the theory the moment it bounded into her head.

"And the resurrection is the miracle," Miles said, "not the crucifixion."

Joskie moaned in approval, ticking his finger at Miles. "That's what's up."

"Okay," said Ira, "whatever that means. But one of those funguses in the crust? That *had* been secured by desert pavement for *millennia?* It gets sent *airborne* by *construction* and causes a *respiratory illness* called—"

"Valley fever," Rose said, "after the Central Valley."

"The kids there are lousy with it," said Fran, stirring a skillet over a camp stove. "Now more than ever with all those Amazon warehouses going in, the data centers. Asthma, pesticides, the exhaust from the trucks coming and going twenty-four hours a day, the whole deal!"

Miles nodded solemnly. "The Central Valley died for our sins."

Rose said, "That Cowschwitz on I-5 gets me every time."

Ira's mouth tightened and twisted. Fran moved on to the lake effect, when migrating birds mistake solar arrays for lakes and try to land there. "Happens all the time at Ivanpah."

"Her girlfriend is the caretaker of Nipton," Rose explained to Miles. "What's her name, Fran? Dilly?"

"Delia," Fran said.

"What's Nipton?" asked Miles.

Joskie gasped. "Magical Nipton!"

"A ghost town pot hotel one valley that way," Fran said, pointing. "Some corporate circus burners just bought it."

"Right by Ivanpah," Rose said. "On the edge of the Mojave Preserve."

"What's Ivanpah?" Miles asked.

Rose's friends stared. "He's new," she said.

"Bech*tel*'s dinosaur solar array," Ira said. "You've probably seen it on the way into Vegas from LA, off the 15. Eye of Sauron–looking towers surrounded by mirrors."

Rose said building Ivanpah had killed eleven hundred tortoises.

"That's just the take," Ira corrected, "just what they had to count. Who knows how many really died." To Miles, he said, "I used to be a bird janitor there. I still have a freezer full of dead birds."

"Ooh," Joskie squealed. "Could I have those for art?"

"These birds," Fran said, "are so exhausted by the time they land at an array, thinking they'd get food and water, that they can't fly away again. And sometimes, when they're landing, they combust in midair. Streakers, they're called. Or streamers?"

"Also"—Joskie again—"and this is fun! Industrial solar uses a shitload of water. Water to wash the panels, to cool the batteries, to keep dust down during construction, which doesn't work."

"And the transmission lines!" said Ira, stomping his empty.

"Roy calls them 'wildfires in waiting,'" Rose said. "Where is Roy?"

"He's coming," Fran said.

"They lose most of the energy made at the array," said Joskie. "Go stand by that transmission line. Not for too long! You can hear the electricity flinging off on its way to the coast."

"Or the Gigafactory," sneered Ira. They were on a roll now, hitting whip-its of confirmation bias. Rose was having the time of her life, except for Miles increasingly left-out and unmoored-looking.

"And the kicker for me," Fran said from the kitchen area, "is this desert—like all intact deserts—"

"Like woodlands," Rose said. "Wetlands, prairies, your forests up north—"

"—was storing carbon."

"*Sequestering* it."

"Saving our asses, in the local parlance."

"Scraping the land *releases* the carbon," said Joskie.

"So, we—" Ira said. "Me and you and Warren Buffett and Joe Brandon and Rex Tillerson—"

"To widely varying degrees," Miles offered feebly.

"—have, in the name of *salvation*, belched a bunch of carbon into the air, sacrificing what BLM *itself* calls 'forest products.'"

"Ira works for them," Rose explained.

"Technically for USGS," Ira amended. "I'm a contractor."

"He's a plant guy."

"I study how invasives affect tortoise foraging."

"How do they?" Miles asked.

"They fuck it up!"

Roy arrived then with a plate of his famous mesquite-flour cookies. They pushed Miles to try one and awaited his verdict. "Delicious," he admitted.

"Superfood." Roy shrugged humbly.

"Anyway," said Ira, "what was I saying?"

"Forest products," Joskie said through a mouthful of cookie.

"That's right. Ninety thousand yuccas!" Ira flung his hands into the air. "*Half a million* creosotes! All the creatures living in, on, and under them!"

"You had your desert night lizards," said Joskie, "snakes, rodents, the only moth that pollinates Joshua trees. The tortoises making burrows for everyone. *Everyone.*"

"Imagine," shouted Fran, shoveling at her sizzling skillet, "the outrage there would be if we mulched ninety thousand sequoias or redwoods for an *in*efficient industrial solar array sending expensive energy to cities—corporations!—far away. We don't have to imagine! The tortoises dug up from their burrows don't have to imagine! Those thirty-some tortoises eaten by badgers don't have to imagine. All this to supposedly save the planet. And in an age of mass extinction!"

Rose said, though she knew Miles knew, "We don't have spare tortoises or disposable swaths of habitat."

"And the irony," Roy offered, his scratchy voice incensed, "is these industrial solar arrays will turn the intact desert into a wasteland when huge parts of it are already wasted."

Rose recited the litany of wasted places. "Military bases, cities, dead agriculture brown fields, parking lots, highways, reservoirs, irrigation ditches . . ."

"All of it," Ira said, "should be sited for solar before we even think of sacrificing another acre of public wilderness."

"Check it out," said Fran, taking her skillet off the camp stove and turning off the blue flames. "If we put solar panels on the parking lots, like they're doing in France, we'd increase solar power capacity by four hundred and fifty percent. And that's not my number—that's not from, from *Jacobin* or some shit. That's *Time* freaking magazine!"

"We can't just switch to a grid that decimates what's left of ecosystems," said Joskie. "It's not only wrong, like, morally—it won't work."

"For-profit industrial solar is just not good enough," said Fran, assembling her signature walking tacos: vegan Soyrizo scooped into fun-size bags of Fritos and topped with yogurt, homemade salsa, and cilantro from Roy's garden.

"There's this false binary between decarbonizing and *biodiversity*," Joskie said, the word dripping with ridicule. "A.k.a. life."

"A devil's bargain," Miles said.

"It's a strategy," Rose said, "and it works—consistently divides the environmentalist community. Are you on the Sierra Club West LISTSERV?"

Miles wasn't.

"Good for you," said Ira. "I'm just waiting for that LISTSERV to die off."

Joskie offered that the only people who should be on that LISTSERV were social scientists studying liberals' internalized despotism. "The only solution anyone on there can come up with, again and again, is—"

Everyone but Miles sang it out: "Population control!"

"They're lining up to man the gas chambers," Roy said, then thanked Fran for the grub.

"Which," Joskie said through a mouthful of walking taco, "aside from the obvious problems"—Ira snorted—"absolutely delights the energy executives."

"Divide and conquer," said Roy.

"But"—Rose now—"our children and grandchildren will not enjoy zipping around in their electric cars if they don't have clean air and water."

Fran presented Rose and Miles with their walking tacos, plastic forks poking out of the Fritos bag, and decried endless growth. "A system that needs ever-increasing amounts of energy extracted from the sacred land that keeps us cannot save us."

"You have to wonder if that is even the goal," Miles said, then of the walking taco, "This is good."

"Right?" said Fran.

Joskie said incremental blunders like Yellow Pine would squander the few years they had left to act.

"Which is the point," said Ira. "A feature, not a bug."

"And even *worse*," said Fran, "I know I keep saying that! It's like every time you think you get to the basement, there's a trapdoor."

"Bottomless greed," Rose said.

"Dead turtles all the way down," Joskie said.

"This path," Fran said, turning back to Miles, "mindless growth, investor-owned utilities—it degrades our collective spirit."

"Say more," said Miles.

"It, like, paves the wild *in us*. We let these guys rape the land and we rape ourselves. I think Bernie said that."

"Sanders?" asked Miles.

"DeVoto," said Fran.

"But we have to do *something*, right?" Miles said. "This is an emergency."

"For sure!" said Fran. "We have to do a bunch of things. But this ain't one of them. Giving public land to Big Tech and energy companies and giving the people who live here nothing—"

"Not a damn thing from either party," Ira said. "So much for hearts and minds."

"We have to be *for* something," Rose said. "What benefit does Yellow Pine give these people? What incentive to cooperate? Extra asthma?"

Joskie groaned in assent. "Liberals haven't given a shit about rural America for decades. And they act surprised when the neo-Nazis run amok."

They lambasted liberals at length.

"Boondoggles like Yellow Pine are just gonna deepen the divide that makes our politics so dumb and dysfunctional," said Fran finally. "And in the process we, like, ransom our *spirit*. For what? Ten jobs? Even BLM admits that Yellow Pine will be 'operated remotely,' 'without permanent staff on-site.'"

Rose added more air quotes from the impact statement. "'Would not appreciably change existing economic conditions in the analysis area.'"

"And the median annual income of an individual in the 'analysis area,' if you're curious," said Ira, "is about twenty-five thousand dollars."

"These executives are the same yahoos who got us into this mess," Rose said. "They will never get us out."

"Not when the government genuflects to them," said Roy.

"We're talking the same industry whose scientists knew in the seventies," Ira said.

"Sixty-eight," said Roy.

"They funded junk science and denier propaganda for decades," said Ira. "They're stalling on renewables to this day!"

"Call me crazy," Joskie said, "but shouldn't the consequences for, I don't know, causing and then *knowingly* profiting from this crisis be more than Thank you, sir. May I have another? Or is everyone in power just totally hunky-dory with all that crime?"

Miles had finished his walking taco. "Steal a little from one person and they call the cops," he said. "Steal a lot from everyone and they make you king. Bob Dylan said that."

Fran clapped a hand to her chest. "Love Bob. But we're beyond him."

"Beyond Bob?" said Roy. "Blasphemy."

"Exactly," said Fran. "This is 'steal everything from everyone and they make you God.'"

"And in the Atacama," Joskie said, "in the global south, the plunder, the carnage—it's a hundred times worse."

They all got quiet. Ira sighed. "Well, now I'm really sad."

Rose too. "So much for the people's solar," she said. So much for what most people think solar power is: clean energy made where it's used, no electric bill. "Everyone wants panels on their roofs now and at best they get rebates."

"Market-based incentives," grumbled Roy. "Financialization."

"Predatory leasing," said Joskie. "Bait-and-switch scams."

"Neoliberalism at its finest," said Ira.

Fran rolled her shoulders back, proclaimed that preserving a livable planet would not be the easiest path nor the cheapest nor the most profitable for executives and shareholders. The floodlights around Yellow Pine blazed on in the dusk. The group fell silent again under their buzz.

"You know what I love about Fritos?" Miles pointed to the nutritional label on the bag. "Corn, oil, salt. Three ingredients. So pure. In this day and age. Can you believe it?"

They couldn't.

Fran needed to check on the sound system. Joskie suggested a visualization exercise first, because "vibrational healing is real." He invited them all to plant their feet and close their eyes. Embarrassing, but Rose did, and (astoundingly) didn't check to see whether Miles did.

Joskie instructed them to imagine shade. "Summon in your mind's eye," he said, "all the melting infrastructure of the Southwest. See it replaced with solar canopies, solar roads. Imagine the millions of people who die early from cancer and pollution still with us, sharing their gifts. Imagine assisting in the birth of a decarbonized economy arranged around interconnectedness and care. Imagine preserving the life-sustaining capacity of these great deserts. Imagine saving the places we go to find ourselves."

Later, beneath a sherbet sunset, there were speeches. Ira talked about the tortoises, then a history professor from the community college spoke, then people from Basin and Range Watch, the Amargosa Conservancy, the Old Spanish Trail Association, and the Center for Biological Diversity.

Fran had made an interpretative sign for the mizpah. Joskie sledgehammered it into the ground. With the origin of the world rising behind her, Fran read the assembled her sign.

With this rock pile we draw a line,
and with that line we honor our elders.

We honor the 92,000 Mojave yucca
and 500,000 creosote destroyed here.

We honor the 139 adult tortoises taken from
their burrows and the 33 killed.

We honor the uncounted tortoise eggs
and young left behind to die.

We honor the soil.

We honor the rocks.

We honor the lichen and the moss.

We honor the kit fox.

We honor the birds.

We honor the insects.

We honor the human.

We honor the coyote.

We honor the cholla and the barrel
cactus and the unknown.

With this rock pile we form a sacred pact
with the living valley. To destroy is the old way.
With this rock pile we enter the new.

Rose started crying at *We honor the human* and didn't stop for a long, long time.

After the speeches, Miles and Roy built a fire. They all sat around it in overcomplicated folding chairs, watching embers pop and firefly up into the darkness. People smoked, roasted marshmallows, laughed, and talked. Rose needled Miles into playing his guitar. He played Joni, Woody, then a song of his own, sung slow and sexily out the side of his mouth. God, the beauty he could make with his breath, with the cords in his throat and six strings stretched across the open mouth of a former tree.

The dark world was brighter beside Miles, more possible. A place where miracles happened all the time. When Miles sang—when he held her, read to her, when they made love or when he made her food or rubbed her back—Rose was set momentarily free of her hatred, her hatred of herself and her country, her chronic full-body disgust for its compulsive consumption, the obscene number of devices per household, the mindless scroll, the greenwashing, the automation, the dehumanization, the constant barrage of bullshit telling people they were wrong and bad and the only way to get okay was to buy more useless shit, which never, ever worked. She said all this and more to a spent, campfire-smelling Miles late that night, squeezed in beside him on the van's narrow bed after excellent sex.

"I hear you," he said. "I feel you. But I'm so tired. I'm sorry, but I can't hear any more about planned obsolesce or cryptobiotic crust today."

"What if we're wrong?" Rose asked.

Miles yawned.

"What if the psychos on the LISTSERV are right? What if this is dangerous? What if we're being rope-a-doped by the enemy? What if . . . what if—I don't know. . . ."

"You can only do your best," Miles said. "Heed your conscience. Trust your gut."

"I know we can't do the right thing out of fear. I keep thinking about how we never talked about how to do it—transition I mean. Transform. It was yes or no, yes or no, for forty years, and now there's no time, they say. But there can't be no time. We have to get this right. People say we can't stop capitalism and climate change at the same time, but I can't see any other way to do it. I'm trying to be unapocalyptic. I'm trying to be practical. It seems practical to me. If we have to rebuild everything anyway, why don't we actually fix it? Cut out the rot. Pull it up by the roots. Couldn't we at least *try* to build some future? I know that sounds abstract, pie in the sky or whatever, but it's real." As concrete as concrete. As simple as shade. "Don't you think? I don't know. Do you think anyone else will care about this place? Do you think any of this will matter?"

Rose waited, listening in the dark, but Miles was asleep.

Many Moons

Back in Tecopa, Rose drunkenly demanded of Miles a timeline.

"When will we make a baby?"

"It's hard to say," he said.

"What's hard to say? What makes it hard?" She could not quit with the questions! She knew it was folly—pathetic! desperate! being-for-death! At the very least foolishly linear, insecure, borderline manipulative. Yet she couldn't stop. Rose thrived in crisis. If she had to create a crisis to thrive, so be it. Very adult child of alcoholics, according to Jane. Miles was understanding of Rose's first half-dozen approaches, then declared himself spent and went home.

"I don't get it," said Lalo, bringing Rose vegan chili at the bar. "I thought you was all eco?"

"I am," Rose told her. "But that doesn't make me antinatalist. Renouncing children delights fossil fuel executives. They invented the carbon footprint to diffuse their responsibility onto all of us. They have created this cult of personal responsibility, demanding the ultimate sacrifice—our future. His and mine! They made us all insane recycling Nazis. The left is no fun anymore. You think I don't want to do LSD in Golden Gate Park? Fat chance! And what have these monsters given up? Nothing. Not one shining penny! I won't make my womb a sacrifice zone."

"Got my tubes tied in the nineties," Lalo said. "But it weren't for tree-hugger reasons. 'Sides, I thought *he* was trying to knock *you* up."

"He was, sort of. Not really. He doesn't love me. Not enough. Not out loud."

"I thought you were wobbly about it. At your age."

"I'm not wobbly. I'm not even forty. I'm sturdy as can be."

Fate and folly looked the same from the outside, Lalo and Rose decided. Exactly the same whether true or false. That's why it was so easy to love foolishly. "But I know me and Miles are fated," Rose told Lalo, having left her sheepishness about Fate on the other side of the portal. "We're in the stars."

"Yep," Lalo said. "And we're made of the same stuff as the stars."

"Exactly!" Rose cried. "And since we're all made of star stuff and the big wheel has been turning for eternity, it makes sense that some people feel like a part of you. Because they *are*. Or were, I guess. Like, maybe my potassium and your potassium were once together in the bones of some fish in Lake Lahontan and when we get close again ten thousand years later at the Rattler Room in Tecopa, our potassium remembers itself from being in the fish and wants to be back together. We're reconstituted. That's how it feels to be back with my kid."

"Yep," said Lalo. She had four, grown and gone. "All like, 'you complete me.'"

"Wholeness," Rose said, desperate for it. "And that's why, if you're lucky enough to find some long-lost potassium of yours, you want more than anything to recombine, reconstitute, maybe make a new being."

"Yep."

"Except it's not new at all," Rose said. "It's been here the whole time."

"Yep," Lalo said again. "In the ether."

Rose granted Miles a one-week moratorium on the subject of their reconstitution. Worst week of her life. "I hate being locked in this dance," she wept on the couch at the end of it. "It's gendered and cliché. I'm not doing it on this side of the portal."

"I don't think it's gendered and cliché," Miles said, rubbing her back. "I think it's important."

"If you're not the person," Rose said, "I need to know."

"I'm not not," he said.

"So you are?"

"I want to be."

"But not yet?"

"Not yet."

"You're not ready yet?"

"I'm not ready yet."

"Maybe you'll never feel ready."

Miles inhaled sharply. "That has occurred to me."

"But that doesn't mean we shouldn't do it. Maybe this is the kind of thing you don't feel ready for before. The kind of thing you can't feel ready for. You get ready by doing it. You take a leap."

"Maybe. But maybe I'm not one of those people. A leaper. I need to feel ready."

"What would make you feel ready?"

"I can't say."

"Are you afraid? What are you afraid of? What're you waiting for?"

Miles was quiet. He sat very still for a long time, staring into the middle distance of the living room. Then he took a deep breath. He was really thinking about it. Tired as she'd made him, Rose marveled, he was hanging in there.

"I am waiting," he said, so slowly, "for the sun to go across the sky some more. I am waiting for a few more moons."

"How many moons?"

Miles looked pained. "I can't say."

"An estimate, then. A guesstimate."

"Many."

"But you just now said *a few*!"

"I know I did."

"Then I pushed you."

"So stop pushing me. You added moons."

"I didn't add moons!" Rose erupted. "I'm not a witch! I don't have that kind of power."

Reverse Clairaudience

Rose woke the next morning alone and profoundly hungover, having stayed up drinking after Miles left and then dreamed about Jane.

"Are you recovering or just abstaining?" Jane had asked in the dream.

"I'm not even sure I'm abstaining anymore," Rose said. "Anyway I thought you were dead." And Jane had laughed a gusting laugh and shook her old glowing head at how mistaken she was.

Rose passed the morning woozily, in an almost-wanting-to-die kind of sickness. She should have gone back to bed but instead seethed at the news on her phone, raging impotently within at every instance of the future tense. Climate change was here now, for everyone. Yet nowhere it seemed was the coronavirus understood to be caused by capitalism steadily euthanizing the planet, by the rich burning up carbon and buffer habitat and flinging novel biota around the world. *When it comes, it will be like this.* This pathetic clinging to anomaly, to analogy, the virus as a preview, a test we're failing spectacularly, rather than seeing that an end, if not *the* end, is here, now.

Vibrational healing is real, Rose tried. She wrote, *The end of the world is not its destruction, but its reinterpretation into heaven,* on a Post-it and stuck it to the fridge. Suppose she reinterpreted this place as heaven. Suppose she considered this a beautiful time. Suppose it were a miracle to be born. Suppose we rebuilt our society around health and peace—close, placed, intimate communities arranged in acknowledgment that we are also animals, soft, hairless, barely upright, and highly permeable animals who need shelter, food, clean water, clean air, other people. Rose wanted only Miles, June, and the new one. When had she become so bereaved? She tried to be abundant, but she only had so much time.

She tried to reject her linear delusions about time. "Peace is real." Juniper said that. Either we stop, turn, and walk toward peace, either we practice peace, or innocent lives continue to end in early, avoidable deaths.

Tomorrow Rose would have circled the sun on this beautiful burning rock forty times.

It was never too late to make a different decision.

Almost never. Rose checked her email and found news that another activist had made an early exit.

Which, God help her, brought Rose back to hope. Not false hope, not Hope™, and for Christ's sake not permission to resume mindless purchasing. Miles had once showed her obligatorynoteofhope.com, a website where some lady described *collective action as the antidote to my dithering and despair. There's a way in for everyone. Aren't you tired of all this fear and dread?*

Rose doesn't know You, but she knows You're tired. If there was any hope, it was blowing up pipelines. Hope was sinking superyachts. Hope was turning the valves. Hope was praying on the prairie while being blasted with the taxpayers' weapons of war. Capitalism got us into this mess, and it would never get us out. American barbarism has come for every living thing on this planet and now it comes for You.

And so what? Countless civilizations have been lost to history. The visible ant work of this time seemed to be single-mindedly driving other creatures and ourselves extinct. (Another word for the latter was *suicide.*)

Rose resolved to say all this in a letter to the Pahrump paper about Yellow Pine, sat down to write it, and was immediately demolished by the pile of books on her table. Writing, for the girl called Sharon, had always been instinctual and pleasurable, sensual and private. She did it for the feeling of the hand moving across the page, the pleasing scratch of the nib against papyrus, the same joyous vibration that put petroglyphs on rocks above springs. Now this hedonism needed to congeal into something more meaningful, if she expected anyone else to be moved by her scratches, expected them to find the spring and drink.

Rose wrote to *The Dusty Trail* about the *I-exist* feeling. Of having made a mark. How our collective mark would outlive our individual marks. Out at Yellow Pine, she wrote, it was impossible to ignore what that collective mark would be. One could, if willing, if possessing the courage, the spiritual mettle, easily identify this civilization's legacy. It was written into the land, and all the easier to read with no trees in the way. See us there in the fossil record? We are not pigment on stone wall or ink on papyrus. Certainly not pixel or code. What we will leave behind after all the rest crumbles is a glowing band of radioactivity and forever chemicals, a toxic swath of highlighter yellow on the map of time, reading, whether we like it or not, YOU WERE HERE.

Rose struggled to mind her dosage. She so badly wanted to have right relationships, *right* meaning good, *right* meaning beautiful, *right* meaning true. When she got brave enough to leave Nothingness Flats, she tried to fall in love with every being she saw, even when it hurt. Especially when it hurt. She wanted to love in a way that hugged hurt, to meet that sensation relaxed and open, not braced against.

Hope was pain was love was sacrifice. There was right sacrifice and wrong sacrifice. Right sacrifice was freedom, it was power—the power to let go, to bear witness, the power to bear anything for a moment: heartbreak, longing, the staggering loss of unfair sacrifice, of an extinction rate ten thousand times higher than baseline, one hundred thousand species gone forever each time this rock circled the sun.

Rose tried to take in these numbers as she wrote, tried, to some extent, to absorb the avoidable carnage. She never would entirely, she knew. She tried to accept the truth, feel her fear and sadness and rage, move through them, *do* something with them. And the doing was ecstatic! There were a million nonarrestable ways to make real hope, to live peace. There are so many of us not hell-bent on self-destruction, and not so many pipelines, engines, valves, or yachts.

Rose emailed her letter to the editor and stood looking out the kitchen window, unsure of what to do with herself. She tried calling Juniper, but no answer. Then she remembered a hand-drawn flyer at the Triangle bulletin board she'd photographed without absorbing. She looked at it on her phone now. In the center was a black peace sign—well, technically a Mercedes logo, but Rose gave the artist the benefit of the doubt. Around that, in the shaky all-caps handwriting of the elderly:

ECO COMMUNITY MEETINGS
CHURCH 3PM SUNDAYS
ALL ARE WELCOME
THERE IS NO PLANET B

What day was it? Sunday. Rose took a nap, gathering the courage to go to the meeting. Miraculously, she went. The only other person there was Pastor Jack, as Rose had expected. Her gut clenched. "You're here," he said, as if they'd discussed it. "Good."

Pastor Jack said a prayer over a stuffed sloth and a candle labeled COEXIST. In the long pause after the prayer, Rose said, "I'm sorry I called the cops on your pot farm. That was stupid."

"Yeah, well." Pastor Jack shrugged, flapped his arms once. "I wish you would have just talked to me."

They settled in, listening to a CD of New Age pan flute and making signs to put up around town. YOU ARE ENOUGH. HANG IN THERE. Corny slogans like that mostly, but making them felt rightly deranged. In her head Rose called them the Deranged Sign-Makers Guild.

She sent Miles the picture of the flyer, and soon he appeared. From the way he and Pastor Jack greeted each other, it seemed this was not Miles's first time at the guild. Miles kissed Rose on the top of her head and settled in with his X-Acto knife, making a giant NOPE stencil to paint over the neo-Nazis' campaign signs.

Rose was not a witch, but she did have power. Power and paid leave. The Club still searched for Topher's replacement—a woman, HR had assured her. Benefits-wise, by American standards she was downright Canadian. Right sacrifice was power, the power to do or to not. The power of refusal, to live better with less. The power to reject wrong sacrifice, to stand against avoidable carnage. The power to wait, to rest, and then to act. Actions were afoot everywhere, the guild reminded Rose, Camp Yellow Pine reminded her, small but meaningful actions, real things that happened, that mattered. The medicine was in the making, the action, the motion, the mark.

Done with their signs, Rose and Miles cleaned up and said goodbye to Pastor Jack. They milled between their cars in the church parking lot, speckled with paint. Miles looked tired, scraped a shoe in the gravel.

"How's training?" Rose asked.

Miles got despondent, bus-driver school having morphed into a bureaucratic ouroboros involving the school district, Caltrans, the Inyo County sheriff, three private contractors (one administering driving tests, the other drug tests, the third a psychological evaluation), the DMV, and the FBI. "And I'm not getting paid for any of it."

"I thought you were."

"I thought so too."

"Fuck."

"Yes, fuck." Miles's whole beautiful body shuddered, and he said, "Care for a soak?"

A storm system had surged up the Sea of Cortez, an atmospheric river slithering over the basin. The last blazing light of day speared through blue and black banks of city-size clouds. Rose and Miles had the Borehole nearly to themselves, the only other car there when they pulled up the Mazda belonging to Georgie Boy, who lived in the bottle house. Georgie Boy was ancient as a bristlecone and largely deaf. He did not need the pretense of interlocution to speak, a great relief to Miles and Rose. They found him holding his daily cigarette effetely above the water and snuggling his slinky terrier mix, Ada, who lived to swim.

"This light!" Georgie exclaimed. "We're in a Maxfield Parrish! It took a whole renaissance to get light like this and we just"—he waved the hand holding the cigarette, sprinkling ash into the water—"walk around in it."

Miles and Rose disrobed and lowered themselves into the hole to soak.

"You know a lotta people think this river's ephemeral," Georgie told Miles.

"Isn't it?"

"No! It's right here!"

"Ephemeral doesn't mean extinct," Miles said.

"Eh?"

"Ephemeral!" Miles shouted. "It means to come and go!"

Georgie shrugged, lifted himself and Ada from the water. Swabbing his drooping genitals, Ada aswirl between his bowed legs, he said, "This place has never been better than it is right now."

Rose tried agreeing, if only for the novelty.

"I'm sorry I said you added moons," Miles said when Georgie and Ada had gone. "That wasn't right. I mean, it wasn't accurate and it wasn't fair. It's just—" He scooped the steaming water into his hands and released it. "You've had these eggs in you your whole life. Your mom made them when you were in her. I don't have anything like that in me. I haven't even *made* the sperm that would be our baby yet."

"It's in the ether," Rose said.

"And your part's here," he said, "on this plane."

"Where I can feel it."

"And you *see* it every month. I mean, it *is* the month. You can see and feel these little planets traveling inside you and then out. I can't feel my balls make sperm. I can feel an orgasm, but that's it. And I know this is all very essentialist and whatever, but, like, on a primitive level there's this—during sex—this fear."

"What fear?"

He looked right at her. "This fear, like: Where did it go? I just disappear in you and my semen—my qi—my essence—spirit—life force—whatever—springs forth! On some level men will never get used to that. We have to give ourselves to you. That's why patriarchy is so bananas with insecurity."

"B-a-n-a-n-a-s."

"I *do* love you," Miles said, getting quiet. "I've loved you for a long time. But I'm scared."

Rose wanted to hold him, but something said wait. She waited.

"I'm scared," Miles said again. "But that doesn't mean I'm not the person. It doesn't mean we weren't a fish."

This place has never been better than it is right now. The idea, the water, and everything Miles had said left Rose spent. Wrung out by writing and praying and amends making and grieving and painting, but ripe with thanks. Like the ending of her favorite ecosocialist elegy, Ross Gay's "Catalogue of Unabashed Gratitude," the ending of which she'd painted on cardboard at the guild.

Soon it will be over,
which is precisely what the child in my dream said,
holding my hand, pointing at the roiling sea and the sky
hurtling our way like so many buffalo,
who said it's much worse than we think,
and sooner; *to whom I said*
no duh child in my dreams, *what do you think*
this singing and shuddering is,
what this screaming and reaching and dancing
and crying is, other than loving
what every second goes away?
Goodbye, *I mean to say.*
And thank you. Every day.

Cloud Report

Rose was not a witch, but she did have power. She turned forty. She willed the moons to come and they came.

One moon brought Miles back to Nothingness Flats. He was ready to try again, he said, he loved her, really loved her, and (this went unsaid) he was broke. The moon saw her letter printed in *The Dusty Trail*, heavily edited but no less rightly deranged.

The next moon summoned to the driveway of Nothingness Flats a scorpion, one of Pastor Jack's sculptures, big as a wheelbarrow and welded from pieces of desks and chairs pilfered from the closed school.

The moon brought Juniper for winter break. Rose, Miles, and June talked regularly on FaceTime, but the three of them together—reconstitution plain as day. Juniper was aggressively hospitable with Miles, insisting he put his bamboo toothbrush in the cup with theirs. Miles amused Rose by being unskilled at imaginative play—too self-conscious to do the voices Juniper demanded. But with a concrete project between them (Lego axolotl, baking soda volcano, Jenga, Uno, bike ride), he was a natural. His true domain was the trampoline, where June screamed, "Launch me to the moon!" and Miles did.

He made himself scarce while June had a meltdown in the aftermath of Christmas morning, squeezed Rose's hand when the kid got sassy, read *Just So Stories* and *Matilda* at bedtime. In their own bed, Miles whispered to Rose how tired he was, how thick time had become, what a good mom she was. On the last day of the visit, June asked if she and Miles could go on a walk down to the river, just the two of them. She came back effervescent, rocks in her pockets, a name and a story for each one, a sparkling avidity Rose had never seen in the kid.

The moon pulled Juniper back across the continent. Miles dropped Rose and June at the Vegas airport at three a.m. then fetched Rose from the same airport again at midnight. He held Rose in the space where June had been.

What it felt like to let her go: the opposite of reconstitution. Blown to bits. Atomization. Painful craving. Longing without the release of action. Like the thing Rose was meant to be doing with her life was not, for almost ten months a year, happening. Like things were not going according to plan. They weren't. Never did, Rose knew. Miles said if this was not her plan, then maybe it was God's. She'd be reconstituted again in three months.

The moon brought more storms, miracle rain, and a call from the superintendent of Death Valley Unified School District. Miles was freed from administrative limbo and could start his route in the new year. The sacrifice zones glowed green with life. The coyotes sang, happy and full of rats. The paper did its part for Operation Plowshare, hysterically reprinting the sheriff's statistics, *X* number of plants confiscated, *Y* number of guns. The involved were ticketed, name and place of origin reported, the deportable deported. The *Trail* printed a picture of a pot farmer outside Olancha, down in a hole where he'd been hiding, looking, Miles said, like Saddam. "For my money, these farmers would need a lot more profit to be in the running for worst people in the world."

Rose, holding the business section, agreed. "At the rate of these returns, Saddam himself wouldn't even rank."

Miles folded away the paper. He gazed unhurriedly out the window. Rose watched him watch. "What about Cloud?" he said after a while.

"Claude?"

"Cloud," Miles said. "For a name."

"Cloud," Rose said. "I love it. But people will think we're saying Claude. They'll think we're snooty."

Miles put his hand to her womb and pressed. "I really don't care what people think."

Unacceptable Apples

Looking back, the beginning of another end for Miles and Rose—in addition to their lopsided love, her doomer tilt, him jumpily moving in with her, then out, then in again, her wanting to have a baby more than he did, both of them mistrusting happiness, both of them getting off on edging toward despair—was the unacceptable apples.

Miles deemed most apple varieties unacceptable. Due to genetic modification, all apples were rapidly deteriorating. Was Rose aware of this? She was not. O, yes: A Fuji may have been an acceptable apple years ago, but it was no longer an acceptable apple. Same with Gala, which Miles considered an affront, same with Honeycrisps ("a disgrace, what the Honeycrisp has become") same with Pink Lady (a "trash apple") same with Jonagold same with EverCrisp same with Jazz.

One had to be ever vigilant, Miles felt, haranguing Rose in the kitchen, had to be forever updating one's apple of choice. Rose admitted the apples Miles brought home to Nothingness Flats were uncommonly delicious: firm, juicy, bright, never dry or mealy. They kept every promise broken by the corporate orchards. And she did not deny that the apples she selected were often off. There was one apple Miles found acceptable presently, but Rose could never remember which. She was just not willing to pour her precious energy into the constant search for ideal apples.

"That's not what I'm suggesting," Miles said, as if she had personally degraded the apple since Eve. "Not at all. I'm not saying go full-on Cosmic Crisp. No one's going to be brought closer to the Source by GMO star skin."

"If that's not what you're saying, then I don't know what you're saying."

Miles looked tired. Maybe miserable. "I am saying we make the choices we have in front of us."

Rose prayed for knowledge of God's will for her, and the power to carry that out. But not only for that.

Salt on the Slug of Her Heart

Philip Roth claimed that when someone said to Chekhov, "This too will pass," Chekov had answered, "*Nothing* passes." Roth pretty much wanted that on his tombstone. That's Newark for you. That's Taganrog for you.

Out here, things passed. People changed, they molted, mutated, let go, were new, rolled on, rode off into the sunset, moseyed on down the dusty trail. Rose believed people could change, really change. Change profoundly! Transformation happened all day every day one day at a time. Or it could. Rose had to believe that, or else she probably could not go on. She was on this side of the portal. She was about what was happening now. So truthfully, she did not give a damn about what had happened between her and Miles the first time around. It didn't matter a whit!

But briefly,

Rose was twenty-one, still an undergrad, Miles was doing his master's in linguistics, slumming in Reno because the university had had a gorilla who could sign and she'd died, and Miles and his adviser were trying to teach her daughters to sign. To their credit, the daughters never did learn.

Miles and Rose met in Spanish class. Miles already knew Spanish—had taken four years of it at his private high school in Portland in a naturally lit classroom named after Frida Kahlo, spent a summer in Ecuador building earth-dome schools with some do-gooder group, lived in Mexico City during his gap year, studied abroad in Barcelona for another year during his undergrad at Reed—but he wanted to brush up for his language exam, so he was auditing. Rose's Spanish immersion consisted of Mexican twin sisters with butthole lip liner bullying her at the bus stop in Pahrump—*chinga tu madre puta* and all that jazz. She was the worst student in the class, Miles easily the best, so for this reason, Rose assumed, the instructor, who'd christened her Rosa, always paired them. Later she found out Miles had in fact asked the instructor, a chum of his, to put them together. She was still going by Sharon then, but on a whim told Miles he could call her Rose.

So fervently crushing on Miles was this brand-new Rose that she overcame her bus-stop-induced aversion and actually studied, practiced, immersed—flash cards, telenovelas, ordering *en español* at Beto's, daring to speak Spanish with her coworkers at the gym and her aunt Angie, the works. By midterm, Rose was dreaming in Spanish of Miles asking her out, which he soon did. They had a spectacular spring spent mostly in bed, emerging only to wash, evacuate, and nibble like squirrels on nuts and dried fruit. Miles fussed about his exams, then sailed through them, off that fall for a fellowship at some Center for Language and Blah Blah Blah at Stanford, an arm of the state (Alice liked to observe) whose real purpose was to launder the reputations of certain American oligarchs for cheap. Rose stayed in Reno to finish her degree, and thus began the time of her life when about all she did was schoolwork, work work, and drive back and forth over the Sierras on I-80 listening to *Silent Spring*.

A towering monument to American denial, the story we tell ourselves about *Silent Spring*. You read the first chapter in high school—even at Rose's school-to-prison-or-war pipeline school they read it. Oh, too bad about the birds in this imaginary place, they say. Would be a such bummer if they stopped singing. Good thing we listened to Rachel and banned DDT.

First of all, the DDT ban took a decade. And we only banned it here. Monsanto, Montrose, Pennwalt, all those assholes went on bukkakeing DDT all over the developing world well after the US ban, long after Rachel Carson broke the bad news. Their subsidiaries make and spray DDT in India to this very day.

Anyway, DDT and birdsong are not the crux of the argument of *Silent Spring*. Cancer is. Specifically, that cancer—cancer at the scale we experience it, which in Rose's day was leagues beyond even what Rachel Carson observed in her time, the middle of the cursed twentieth century—is new, largely man-made, preventable, avoidable, optional. It takes her several chapters to build to her argument about cancer, and who can blame her for having to gird her loins, given the shitstorm that she rightly knew would rain down on her head, and given she herself was dying from it, but finally Carson depicts humanity at a crossroads.

Path the First: Stop inventing chemicals we don't need: *500 new chemicals to which the bodies of men and animals are required to somehow adapt each year, chemicals totally outside the limits of biologic experience*. Quit with the splitting of the atom and such insanity, and actually *prevent* cancer. Make it illegal to poison every living thing for money, basically.

Path the Second: Don't fuck with the bottom line. Accept cancer as an inevitable force of nature rather than an invention, the very specific mistake of progress it is. Don't question the god of profit. Focus on treatment.

Guess which path appealed to America's titans of industry? To the ever-respectable medical sector's academies and associations? As Rose saw it, as Rachel saw it, given the choice between a bonanza of optional poisons and slightly less profitable cancer prevention, we went all in on pink ribbons.

This thinking fruited in Rose as she hurtled across the fabulously abused landscape we call the American West, chasing Miles their first time around. If you want to get purchase on the cultural differences between Northern California and Northern Nevada, drive back and forth over the Sierras on I-80 for a year. Westbound, it's all in front of you: a land of possibility, a place with a future. Zip through Donner Pass, tip your hat to the obelisk beside the freeway stretching nakedly to the height the snow was that winter in 1848 when the Donners ate each other. Won't have that problem again anytime soon! Slalom down the western Sierras and let the Yuba River, slick as destiny, float you home. Unless you're paying a certain kind of very close attention, which is to say unless you are into BDSM of the soul like Rose of Sharon Williams, you can't tell that the "palisades" of the Truckee meadows are in fact humongous scrape scars from Gold Rush 2.0, hydraulic mining edition, gaping wounds where so much mountain was blasted away that the debris slurry rinsing downstream raised the whole Sacramento River Delta by half a foot.

Eastbound, from the Bay back to Reno, you can't miss the butchery. The animal stink outside Davis, the mosquito swarms rising from the instant swamps of Sacramento. Bleak industrial wineries, skeletal orchards, windowless warehouses. Then the Sierra foothills forcing you to slow down enough to take in the corridor's eerie manmade wrongness. This last segment of I-80 spans the codependent personalities of the two regions—the Bay Area's arrogance, Nevada's low self-esteem. Westbound, the settler arrives in the Bay at an angle of divine repose. Eastbound, she is, as the OG Nevadans were, California backwash.

Rose had fallen deep in love with Miles, and it changed everything. Being backwash, Rose of Sharon hadn't known herself capable of—worthy of—a love like theirs. She was still a little wobbly about it to this very day, if she was being honest. The worthiness deal.

Now, after over half a decade uncoupled and arrived at middle age, Rose had some inkling as to where she got this mistaken conviction. From being a poor kid in a rich country. What wasn't baked into her cracked family system she picked up at work: retail and food service and the front desk of 24 Hour Fitness in Reno. Unlovability, expendability, they clung to her like a stink, like radioactive ash. Driving back and forth over the mining-molested Sierras and given the choice between listening to Alice or listening to Rachel, Rose vastly preferred Rachel. She'd roll up to Miles's graduate student housing smelly and enraged from another round of *Silent Spring,* and they'd talk about it. They'd talk the terror away.

Then one night, honoring an unknown urge, Rose drove to Stanford unannounced. She arrived late, still in her 24 Hour Fitness uniform, and eased quietly into Miles's dark apartment. He must have been asleep. Rose remembered feeling glad for him, and relieved for her, because Alice had called Rose at work that day, was suicidal again, and Rose wouldn't have to tell Miles about it until the morning. But she didn't end up telling him, then or ever, because Miles was asleep in bed with someone else. Someone from his program. Another brilliant linguistics fellow. Rose looked her up later. A science-of-the-mind person named Rachel. Ouch, ouch, ouch.

Rose turned around and drove back to Reno, decidedly not careening her car off the freeway into the so-called palisades as the sun came up over Donner Lake and vowing instead to never see or speak to Miles ever again.

Rose got stuck in her sorrow. She needed it. Hits of righteous injury displaced her girlhood woes and dysfunctional family dramas.

Bitterness got her through the night shift, where her only other company was a trickle of sex workers doing compulsive cardio and the bleak job prospects for a twenty-first-century English major. A sugar high of hurt feelings kept her from returning Miles's calls or accepting his apologies, as did invasive thoughts of having humiliating sex with him and this Rachel person, who in Rose's mind had become Rachel Carson. Rose was in her early twenties, mistook self-pity for self-respect, overstated harm, nursed resentment, ruminated on betrayal as a relief from the facts of forever chemicals, cancer clusters, and graduation.

Then, some months into this completely ordinary infidelity fiasco, Rose's dad died. Impulsively she asked Miles to come to Kona for the funeral, and he did. He was by her side the whole week, running interference with Alice, with Jim's mentally ill relatives and his emotionally stunted AA buddies, all of them determined to inform Rose how Jim not telling any of them that he was sick was actually her fault.

By the end of the week, Rose cupped a flickering hope that she and Miles would get back together, but Miles had the courage to end it cleanly. They each retreated to their Rachel. Rose took hers to graduate school, where she wrote a sturdy, sincere, if short, sloppily cited, and scholastically unfashionable thesis about the literature of life after death, muscled her way into marriage and waited around to have a baby.

She did not let herself think of Miles much during the blurry, lonesome years of early motherhood, except accepting an algorithm's matchmaking them, then promptly muting him. If she entertained even the most passing thought of him, Rose knew, she'd be in the muck again.

Enough is enough, as Fran liked to say. Miles's parents were lawyers, good ones—his mom sued polluters and his dad was a public defender. They had enough. Having enough without doing harm—enough and not a smidge too much—was freedom. Lucky Miles. You would not find him on the night shift wiping down exercise equipment with chemicals the color of a dangerously dehydrated person's pee. Miles you would find at Mount Hood Montessori in northeast Portland, in classrooms named after Frida Kahlo and Rachel Carson. You'd find him at a cozy liberal arts college making up a major, debt-free and mushroom hunting in the forest, seed harvesting in the rain shadow, counting birds or trimming pot when he needed money, reading library books in a hammock hung in an ancient grove, plumbing the depths of consciousness and language in the great works of great men, an extremely free boy dangling from El Capitan without a rope.

Rose didn't need all that to feel alive. For that she had death.

Shortly before Juniper was born, Rose's lump of a stepdad left Alice at last, for a real-estate broker who'd renamed herself Chloë, with the umlaut, and was making a killing selling groundwater rights. Rose watched heartbreak and rejection settle atop Alice's depression, dispossession, and exhaustion, another loss dredging every other loss to the surface again, another confusing, coerced forfeiture in a long life of them. So embarrassing, how much Chace's leaving hurt Alice. How it made her into a little girl. Chace was a loser, an NFL fanatic, a degenerate gambler, a Tea Party Republican. Still, Alice went off the rails. She threw herself headlong into drinking, became devoted to her suffering, married to her grievances the way a nun was married to God.

Four years after he'd left his body and two-and-a-half decades after she'd left him, Alice fell in love with Jim all over again. She'd call Rose, slurring stories about how beautiful the years on the mango farm had been before Rose's arrival, though Rose knew from Aunt Angie that Jim was a lout, had cheated on Alice *todo el tiempo* back in the day. If in these talks Alice found Rose insufficiently sympathetic, she would beg then demand her daughter return to Pahrump, saying Rose had abandoned her, that she was selfish, ungrateful, that she'd been that way since she was a little girl, had always thought she was better than everyone, fancy college girl studying *lit-rah-ture*, brat with a master's who couldn't even take care of her own mother. There was no food in the trailer, Alice said. If Rose knew so much, had such a big brain, read such big books, did she even know that her own mother was starving? Did she even care?

Rose did know. She remembered hunger. Remembered it from Pahrump, had gotten a second summer job, nights after lifeguarding all day, at a pizza chain to get food. She remembered intentionally screwing up a pizza whenever she could get away with it in hopes the manager would let her take it home. She remembered flirting with a delivery boy so he would leave a box of BO-smelling chicken wings on the passenger seat of her car and tell the customer oops, he'd forgot them. She remembered shoving cold pepperoni into her apron pockets and then into her mouth in the walk-in freezer, which she never wanted to do ever again.

She knew. Caring was another thing entirely, Rose learned when she moved back, dragging her small, sun-shocked family with her. So it went until the night Alice slipped off her back steps and onto another plane.

Once, up at the mine on Mount Tecopa and despite their agreement to be on this side of the portal, Miles asked Rose about her divorce. "How did it go for you?"

"Mainly I was relieved."

"Did it hurt?"

"Sure. But that was the relief. The pain gave me some sort of . . . atonement?"

"Atonement," Miles said. "Interesting idea. At-one-ment. Bringing the pieces back together. Did you try couples therapy?" Miles and his ex had done heaps.

"I didn't think it would work. I didn't want it to work. But also I had other reasons."

"What reasons?"

"I was acting on a hunch."

"What hunch?"

"That they'd be better off without me."

"Were they?"

"He was. Is." Will seemed happy in Philly.

"And her?"

"I think it's better for her like this, yeah. For now. That's how bad it was. But is she better off without me? No. I don't think so. Not anymore. It hurts her. I know that. That's why she's so mad at me. That's why she doesn't like me."

"I don't think she doesn't like you." Miles tossed a rock. It clanged against the grate covering the mouth of the mine and fell into the abyss. "That's just a story you're living in," he said. "A bad hunch."

They'd often terrified Rose, her visions, her whims, her hunches. The urgency she'd felt to conceive Juniper, how desperately she'd wanted to make her, the mistakes she'd made to do it, the carnage in her wake. But today she saw that heeding that craziest hunch was the best decision she'd ever made.

Still, she wondered, what was the rush? Maybe she'd been trying to catch Jim on a round of reincarnation. Looking into Juniper's eyes for the first time the day she was born, Rose saw she'd missed. Thank God. Juniper was entirely her own.

During the years Rose spent dismantling her marriage and building herself a new life—both an ordinary midlife crisis and the second most exhilarating act of creation she'd ever undertaken—Rose did not allow herself to even think of Miles, kept him psychically muted, did not respond to the texts he sent every year on her birthday. She couldn't forgive herself for losing him, for loving him and not being brave enough to tell him. For this reason in the years before, during, and after her marriage, Rose viciously compared any romantic prospect that came her way to Miles, unable to see the typically totally decent person in front of her. Compare and despair, as they said in the program. After her divorce Rose stumbled into bed with one or two adequate not-Mileses and a bunch of true losers before swearing off others entirely. Minus her time with June, Rose was alone, usually contentedly, with the occasional trough of despair brought on by endless war, self-harm on a geologic scale, or plain old loneliness. Things she had never been able to talk about with anyone but Miles.

Why was Miles so sticky for Rose? The best answer she had for that was Portland, Oregon. There is a thick spiritual cord running from the rainforests of the Pacific Northwest down the Cascades and the Sierras to the oases of the Mojave. The ancients could swim between them. Tree people from up north came down to the desert to dry out and get clear; desert rats fled to the forest for rain, shade, shelter. Portland was desert-rat Valhalla, though Rose lived unknowingly at the base of her own Olympus.

All to say Rose felt vast unseen psychic forces tethering her to Miles. No one understood her like him. No one else could rappel down into her gloom and if not pull her out, keep her company. By swearing him off, she thought about him all the time, for years and years and years. When she bought Nothingness Flats, it was Miles she'd fantasized would live there with her. By the time he moved in she could barely see him.

Everyone is here now.

What was she supposed to do with that?

Rose wondered now if she ever saw Miles, ever saw him as he truly was. Probably not. She was seeing Frida Kahlo and Rachel Carson. She was seeing the wide, roiling Columbia, the rivers Yuba and Truckee, worshipping them, blinded by the shimmering peek a boo halo of Mount Hood. She was seeing Juniper and the new one up in the sky islands, shaded by an impossible forest of junipers, Joshuas, redwoods, pines, and firs, none of them burning. Or if burned, coming back. This she saw without seeing.

When the covid dome came down, Rose had felt instantly less alone. Everyone had to stop what they were doing. Everyone saw they could not keep walking the path they were walking. Everyone's vision was now touched with death. Rose's word was *welcome*.

On this side of the portal, much of what made sense to Rose back on the other side now made no sense. Now looked plainly insane. She wanted to do nearly none of what she had been doing for about a decade. But those few things that still made sense to her made sense with her whole being: Juniper. Tecopa. Yellow Pine. While the world counted bodies, Rose drove up and down the mountains, across the blasted valleys, following a black line through the molested desert lonesome for a voice. She'd return to Nothingness Flats smelly and outraged at another futile public-comment period, another array fast-tracked, another round of *Silent Spring* on audiobook, convinced herself killable and riddled with tumors.

But now, miraculously, Miles was there. Reading, tinkering, cloud watching. He'd hold her, shower with her, and then take her to bed. Falling asleep, she'd think, *At least I've said what needs saying. Whether he loves me back or not, whether we make a baby or not, at least I've been brave. At least I don't feel like that sort of heel anymore.*

The sort of heel she was was the sort that still couldn't see Miles, even now, after all these years, all these retreats and returns, all these thresholds and voices, the stinging mistakes and wild, unforeseen joys. We can never see without the scrim of ourselves, and it's ourselves we see least of all. Even now, after so much transformation, so many burned ranges and changed names, two scrubbed souls on the cusp of bringing forth a brand-new human being called Cloud waiting in the ether, Rose would probably never see Miles fully—wouldn't even want to.

Just how little Rose saw of Miles became plain when he came home to Nothingness Flats one evening after his route, trembling.

Rose said, "I made risotto."

Miles said, "I need to end this. I need to move out."

"Again?" What about transformation? What about the new one? What about heaven? "What about our future? What about all this insemination role-play?"

"That's exactly what it was," Miles said. "*Play.* Fantasy."

"What about not not trying?"

"Not not trying is hardly trying," Miles said, more mad at himself, it seemed, than anything. "It's not even barely trying. It's less than the bare minimum. Like, we say we might want to have a baby, then we go soaking, which apparently sperm-wise is pretty unwise."

"What are you talking about?"

"The hot water. It zaps them."

"Did you *know* that?"

"Not really. Kinda? There's something unconscious there. Some block."

"What about Cloud?" Rose wanted to know.

Miles looked down into his hands. "Cloud was . . . a fever."

A trapdoor in the floor of Rose swung open. Everything she thought she knew plummeted down to the hot molten center of the earth. "You don't mean that."

Miles did. He said she'd swept him away. At first Rose took this as a compliment. It wasn't one. He meant swept away the way a flash flood swept you away, as in to your early death. He said he was afraid of losing himself, and then he cried. That softened Rose. She knew it wasn't easy to be the leaver. She loved him; she didn't want him to lose himself. If he was lost to himself, he'd be lost to her too. He already was.

Miles said he still wanted her in his life, that he didn't want to lose her again. Rose said she felt the same. Later, she wished they'd stopped there, but they didn't.

Miles lamented his inability to give Rose everything she wanted. He made it seem like she wanted so much, like it was all she did, all she was: a want hole. He said he could barely give himself what he needed. He said being with her was like a bad trip, a runaway train. He said he was so confused. He said he could not tell if he was acting out of love or fear. He said she was a ride he had to get off.

"So get off, then," Rose said, letting the broken screen door slam and leaving him to pack. As she told Lalo and the brewmaster at the Rattler Room that night, quite drunk, more sorrow seeping in, agony achurn in her guts, "I don't want to be anybody's Mr. Toad's Wild Ride."

When she got back, he was gone again. She dreamed a black egg. In the morning, she double-checked her moon glyphs and confirmed. Her period was a week late.

Bit of a Pickle

Rose's plan, the day Miles once again poured salt on the slug of her heart, had been to tell him the suspected great news about her late period. Honestly, he should've known something was up when he came home and found her aglow in an apron, making risotto and listening to R&B. But instead of Rose setting steaming plates of abundance on the table and announcing, "I think I'm pregnant!" and them boning in celebration, Miles had bailed again, as Rose should have known he would, and the risotto burned on the stove.

What surprised Rose, crumpled on her couch the next morning, sicker than she'd ever been, eating cold, burnt risotto from the pan, was this newcomer, the relief. A release, an evaporation of a distinct disquiet that she had not, until then, allowed herself to feel, but which had nonetheless been dragging on her. After so much bracing for impact, she could at last relax. She could rest. She could reel. She could admit to herself, if only to herself, that she needed more solidity, more love, the feeling, the force, the word. Needed a love more mountain than sand dune.

She was heartbroken for sure—racked with grief. But at some point, she lifted her greasy head and noticed she was still here. The plants were still here, the creosotes, the olive, the pomegranate, the palms. It was late February, Mojave spring, and the desert thrummed with life. Lizards suntanning on the deck, spazzy mourning doves nesting in the pergola. She showered, hiked up to the mine to check on the yucca family, discovering as she walked something curious about this strain of heartbreak: It was middle-aged. With a sliver of detachment, its intensity was almost pleasurable. Against being orphaned, away from her kid almost ten months a year, and watching the land she loved ruined for no good reason, to be dumped was no tragedy. At forty years old, Rose knew best practices called for space and time apart to reset.

After her hike, she wrote Miles an email:

Dear M,
Thank you for telling me what you're going through.
That was brave. I don't want to lose you either. You're
important to me. The most important adult in my
life. I walk around with you in my head. You make
me more in love with the world.

She deleted that. Wrote something to the effect of I should tell you that it's possible I am currently pregnant. Deleted that as well.

You're important to me, she wrote. I respect your decision to end us again. I need some time, maybe about a month, before I can move into a friendship with you, which I hope to do.

Yrs,

Deleted that.

Sincerely,
R

Friendship. She'd never exactly mastered it. Rose had friends, but having locked herself in love jail with Miles, she'd neglected them. Still, she'd been blessed by a life of many crises and losses and knew enough to lean on other people, finding she had many who could lean on her when life sucker punched them. When Joskie told her, beside the fire at Camp Yellow Pine, of his older brother who'd overdosed and how it had knocked him out of orbit ever after—or Fran around that same campfire plunged headfirst into her overwhelming disillusionment with academia, its solipsism and cowardice and complicity, the learned helplessness of the professoriate, her fear of being contaminated by it, her deeper fear of being rejected by it, not even having the chance to be contaminated—or Ira admitted to the rage roiling deep in him at all times, that he never felt so alive as he did in Rojava, or brawling against the Proud Boys in Berkeley—or Roy in his old froggy voice told how since his Shelly had passed, he sometimes wasn't sure he wanted to be here (*here* here)—Rose was unafraid of their suffering. And when they inevitably apologized for these disclosures, beat retreat from them, she could say, and mean, "No. Go on. I can bear it."

Rose loved these people the way she loved the tortoises, the yuccas, the desert pavement. (She wanted a better term for desert pavement. Fran would have one. Pavement was a disgusting material, an engineering blip, Goddess willing. The beautiful formation of interlocking stones the soulless scientists called desert pavement was an artwork the earth made over thousands of years, the opposite of asphalt sludge rolled flat by a machine, of the stinking slurry of modernity dumped down in a moment. Desert pavement was a super-long-term performance piece by wind and rain, a sculpture of deep time.) Rose leaned on her Yellow Pine friends, and they leaned on her. Together they made a rock.

Miles was different. She didn't love him like a tortoise or a rock or a friend. She loved him like the beautiful, brilliant cloud-watcher he was. He'd single-handedly restored her faith in the future. She'd seen a life with him, and now that life was gone. Yet it wasn't entirely gone. For one, an important part of it was possibly still inside her. The idea rewarmed a stale metaphor. Rose's torch was more like a guttering votive, and maybe its wick was denial—time would tell. Still, the flame of hope burned inside her.

More empirically, Miles wasn't *gone*. He was not only still on this earthly plane and verifiable, but a short walk down Arroyo Road, his van parked again at Pastor Jack's casita. He wanted to be friends. Could Rose do that without clinging to the threshold? He was plainly the love of her life. She could not pretend otherwise. She'd already been crushed by him once and reconstituted. Worth a shot.

First, she needed to lick her wounds and work her program. She detoxed from her craving one day at a time, replacing Miles's cloud reports with Mary Austin's:

> *Weather does not happen. It is the visible manifestation of the Spirit moving itself in the void. . . .*
>
> *Days when the hollows are steeped in a warm, winey flood the clouds came walking on the floor of heaven, flat and pearly gray beneath, rounded and pearly white above. They gather flock-wise, moving on the level currents that roll about the peaks, lock hands and settle with the cooler air, drawing a veil about those places where they do their work. If their meeting or parting takes place at sunrise or sunset, as it often does, one gets the splendor of the apocalypse. . . .*
>
> *Sometimes one has the good fortune from a heather-grown headland to watch a rain-cloud forming in midair. Out over meadow or*

lake region begins a little darkling of the sky, —no cloud, no wind, just a smokiness such as spirits materialize from in witch stories. . . .

From Kearsarge, say, you look over Inyo and find pink soft cloud masses asleep on the level desert air; south of you hurries a white troop late to some gathering of their kind at the back of Oppapago [the Weeper]; nosing the foot of Waban [the Mountain], a woolly mist creeps south. In the clean, smooth paths of the middle sky and highest up in air, drift, unshepherded, small flocks ranging contrarily. You will find the proper names of these things in the reports of the Weather Bureau—cirrus, cumulus, and the like—and charts that will teach by study when to sow and take up crops. It is astonishing the trouble men will be at to find out when to plant potatoes, and gloze over the eternal meaning of the skies. You have to beat out for yourself many mornings on the windy headlands the sense of the fact that you get the same rainbow in the cloud drift over Waban and the spray of your garden hose. And not necessarily then do you live up to it.

Thus did Rose beat out for herself many mornings on the windy headlands the sense of the fact that she was probably pregnant and freshly dumped by the father of her unborn child—bit of a pickle. *And*, also, how feminist and bohemian! Rose found she loved the idea of being pregnant and not anyone's wife or girlfriend, decided it the path of the Goddess. She had no morning sickness and took this as a good sign from the new one, plain as a rainbow from a garden hose.

Rose knew women who had had babies without partners, or knew of them. A guy she'd met at Standing Rock got a girl pregnant there and she had it without him. Rose wasn't an idiot. She knew she couldn't do it alone, but she wasn't alone. She had friends, her program, her neighbors. Lalo, the brewmaster, Travis the baker, Pastor

Jack. Every Sunday it seemed brought a newcomer to the guild: a warm snowbird potter named Annie, a fabulous young graphic designer from New York named Paki, a severe Gen-X photographer named Cam and her wife, Marcy, a former editor of *Ms.* magazine who lived together in a refurbished shipping container at the hot springs campground. Maybe it was a great time to have a baby. Maybe it had never been better than it was right now. It seemed possible that the fabric of society was mending somewhat, if only thanks to the sheer tensile strength of American repression. Whether those sutures held or not, Rose vowed to enjoy the interregnum.

She cranked up the phone-a-friend tree, bared her soft underbelly, shared her tale of woe for all who'd listen, asked after everyone's No Early Exits Mental Health Action Plans. She journaled her ass off, recorded her dreams, meditated, soaked at the Borehole and the county baths, did yoga every day no matter what. She ignored Miles's school bus when she saw it around town, hiked to the mine weekly, kept going out to Yellow Pine to see Fran and pray at the mizpah. Her suffering was a moment, a moment in the American West. It would pass. It was only a matter of time, the simplest question answered in the oldest way: the sun moving across the sky.

Four or five arcs of craving, a week tops. Thirty days to rewire the brain. Rose quit drinking, grew new synapses, walked the Goddess path without distraction. Over the course of her detox, she noticed that her sadness, if left alone, passed with surprising quickness, like hurrying clouds. She did not look further into this hot-water-zapping-sperm business. She bought a pregnancy test but didn't take it. She had the right to sit with the situation on her own awhile, she reasoned. There was really no point in taking the test until she was ready to tell Miles, and no point in telling him until she had decided what to do for herself. Miles knew how babies were made. He had made his choices and Rose would make hers, her body her choice, which she knew Miles believed.

On day thirty-one of detox, Rose accepted Miles's offer to become friends and joined him on a trash walk. She worried she'd be overwhelmed with horniness being around him, but found she wasn't. She didn't even want to smooch him, though their goodbye squeeze left her high for days.

From there they hiked regularly, often made each other dinner after, hangs Rose found only mildly fraught and then, in time, not fraught at all. She wouldn't, couldn't, tell Miles about the new one yet, but she let it slip to Juniper on FaceTime.

"I think I am going to have a baby."

"I already knew that," June said.

"You already knew that?"

"Yes," the kid said, baldly annoyed. "I can also predict the weather. It's because I'm Latina."

Weather does not happen. That night Rose lay in bed listening to the wind, the Spirit moving in the void, feeling for the new one. She felt witchily confident Miles would accept her decision with kindness. He would be happy. So happy they might get back together. All the while her blood stayed in. Test or no test, she was making a being.

No Early Exits

TWELVE-PRONGED NO EARLY EXITS MENTAL HEALTH ACTION PLAN (JANE)

1. We admitted we were powerless over alcohol—that our lives had become unmanageable.
2. Came to believe that a Power greater than ourselves could restore us to sanity.
3. Made a decision to turn our will and our lives over to the care of God *as we understood God.*
4. Made a searching and fearless moral inventory of ourselves.
5. Admitted to God, to ourselves, and to another human being the exact nature of our wrongs.
6. Were entirely ready to have God remove all these defects of character.
7. Humbly asked God to remove our shortcomings.
8. Made a list of all persons we had harmed, and became willing to make amends to them all.

9. Made direct amends to such people wherever possible, except when to do so would injure them or others.

10. Continued to take personal inventory and when we were wrong promptly admitted it.

11. Sought through prayer and meditation to improve our conscious contact with God *as we understood God,* praying only for knowledge of God's will for us and the power to carry that out.

12. Having had a spiritual awakening as the result of these steps, we tried to carry this message to others, and to practice these principles in all our affairs.

TWELVE-PRONGED NO EARLY EXITS MENTAL HEALTH ACTION PLAN (LALO)

1. my kids
2. the Rattler Room
3. weed
4. gardening
5. eating leafs
6. helping others
7. creosote branch on the shower head
8. b vitamin shots
9. incense
10. a clean house
11. prayer
12. divorce

TWELVE-PRONGED NO EARLY EXITS MENTAL HEALTH ACTION PLAN (PASTOR JACK)

1. Hambone
2. Stu
3. Jesus
4. justice
5. art
6. mountains
7. rock hounding
8. my mom
9. near beer
10. the Niners
11. my garden
12. my ministry

TWELVE-PRONGED NO EARLY EXITS MENTAL HEALTH ACTION PLAN (FRAN)

1. Yellow Pine
2. poems
3. the Borehole
4. writing press releases
5. teaching
6. sun worship
7. walking
8. my family
9. the county baths
10. mizpahs
11. early American transcendentalism
12. Nipton

TWELVE-PRONGED NO EARLY EXITS MENTAL HEALTH ACTION PLAN (IRA)

1. the foamy green beards the tortoises get when they eat
2. the way tortoises climb on top of each other when they eat
3. the way they fall off each other
4. long drives or hikes encountering zero other people
5. Yellow Pine
6. Double Negative
7. tattoos
8. Gramsci
9. Hegel
10. direct action
11. comrades
12. punk

TWELVE-PRONGED NO EARLY EXITS MENTAL HEALTH ACTION PLAN (JOSKIE)

1. my kids
2. my lovers
3. artmaking
4. Ifa
5. jazz
6. vibrational healing
7. Black cowboys
8. kindness
9. the desert
10. the ancestors
11. dancing
12. clowning

Dream Journal

Rose dreamed Philip Roth was her boyfriend. Theirs was a long-distance relationship conducted entirely over the phone. Chekhov was Roth's nurse, helped him with the phone. Roth was an affectionate boyfriend, very loving and supportive, but also intimidating. Rose had doubts about their future.

Rose dreamed she was in *My Nurse and I,* in which Frida is both a breastfeeding baby and the nurse she suckles from, whose face is a mask of a pre-Columbian goddess. The white milk dripping from the nurse goddess's breast, the white lace of baby Frida's gown, the white veins of the engorged leaf behind them, the white rain. In the dream, Rose was the rain.

Rose dreamed of walking with Miles at Yellow Pine. The panels and fences were gone or not up yet. She was huge with the new one, and Miles was happy. They walked by a shipping container. A worker came out with a length of metal pipe in one hand and in the other a selfie stick with a phone on it. He came at them. Miles picked up a wrench. The worker shoved the phone in Rose's face. "Look how fat she's gotten, everyone." He angled the camera at her ass. "She's really let herself go." Rose lunged at him, trying to knock the phone away. Miles hung back, his hand with the wrench at his side. Rose wanted Miles to put himself between her and the worker, wanted him to take her hand, to wrap her in his long arms and spirit her to safety, but knew he would not. Knew no cavalry was coming. To Miles, Rose said, "You better go call the cops." Miles went. Rose was alone with the worker. She turned to face him, then woke up.

Rose dreamed Miles stood barefoot on a dead patch of dirt surrounded by barbed wire. *Don't move don't move don't move.* Carefully, she removed the wire.

Rose dreamed the black egg cracked open and woke up bleeding. No pain, but undeniably bleeding. The unmistakable oxidized iron color of menses.

Menses, Latin for months.

So she is forgiven for thinking, *Time is running out.*

Sperm Wars

The trapdoor again. The plummet to the center of the earth. Not being pregnant after all made things simpler, Rose told herself, trying to rally. Not so bohemian, not walking the Goddess path, but simple. Simple could be good. Simple could work for her. She had over forty days of emotional sobriety, had earned her chip, in her case a new tattoo. She took some Midol and stayed in bed with a heating pad. She wept, grieved, booked a massage in Shoshone. She felt heavy. Weighed down. Low. She sensed into her tissues, felt them detaching, her uterus shuddering, her cesarean scar snag. She felt the throb of the recent past leaving her, its memories and accumulated experiences all dropping out of her. She swirled her menses in their neoprene cup, examining the remnants of Miles, the last of his material within her now released. Rose saw a lot of sorrow in the swirl, and a lot of strength. This was the primordial ooze, the place we all began. This was the stuff she'd grown inside her while getting free, while digging in, while taking it easy, while tending the flame of hope, while asking for help. This liquid tissue was time, the time when she'd made space in herself for calm and contemplation, found a middle setting, discovered the whole wide continent of experience that lay between the coasts of mania and dead inside. It was wild, beautiful stuff, and she poured it into the toilet.

Two nights later, Miles came over for dinner. Rose made risotto. This time Miles intuited the portent right away.

"What's wrong?"

"I got my period."

He blinked at her.

"It was late," Rose said, "really late. And I thought . . ."

Miles blinked more, swallowed, then said, "I'm sorry." He stood and gave her a squeeze. "I know you really wanted it. You must be sad."

In his arms, Rose thought about how that sentence could mean *I assume you are sad* or *It is vital that you be sad*. Either way she was sad all right. Yet like the grown-ass, emotionally mature, semirecovering middle-aged woman she was—or like any preschooler familiar with the film *Inside Out*—Rose felt aswirl with many feelings at once. Sadness and relief. Loss and gratitude. Regret and blessedness. Denial and acceptance. She prayed only for knowledge of God's will and the power to carry it out.

Plus: She already had a baby! She could foster or adopt. "There are all sorts of ways to have kids in your life. I know that," Rose said, though she didn't yet feel it.

"The world is full of children needing love," Miles said.

"I know," said Rose. "You don't have to make a fetus with your body to love the children of the world, to love the world." That's what she'd been trying to do this whole time! *No duh, child in my dreams*, what do you think all this fucking and crying and walking and sign making is?

Still, Rose was bummed. Profoundly bummed. But it was okay to be bummed, she knew. To be bummed was sacred. Even down in the pit of despair, Rose knew that was where all the meaning was. Knew a life that had her feeling so deeply was as good as it got.

Miles agreed. "Sure beats the alternative."

"And it's nice," Rose said through snotty sniffles, "not to have to fill out any insurance paperwork."

"Always nice to avoid an encounter with HR." Miles touched her bicep, turning it slightly to see her new tattoo, a creosote sprig in flower. "A new one." His touch a drug. "Beautiful."

Miles stayed with Rose until she was ready for bed. In bed Rose found she wasn't tired. She went to the Rattler Room. Lalo wasn't there. Rose had never been there when Lalo wasn't there, and she'd never been there so late. Some sort of military-police footrace was passing through—the "hog trot," the brewmaster called it. The place was teeming with the athletic enlisted, an atmospheric river of testosterone. Rose made small talk with Cam and Marcy, said hello to Travis the baker and his wife, who was pregnant and having a root beer. Out on the patio, Rose tied one on, downing pint after pint of heavy ale and smoking nearly a pack of cigarettes while entertaining fantasies of a gangbang atop the pool table. Just when she thought she might need to go to the bathroom to masturbate or throw up, a young man in combat boots and a high-and-tight came outside and asked her for a light. Rose estimated him to be twenty-one-years-and-one-day old. Very virile. The ashtrays were overflowing.

Rose passed the young Marine her lighter. He lit his cigarette and hers, her last. She told him that if they were in an old movie, this would mean that they would fuck.

"Hays Code," he said, surprising her.

"That's right," Rose said. Then, "What percentage of people do you think are not actually sired by the man they think is their father?"

"Sired?" He shrugged. "No idea. Two?"

"It's ten."

"In the US or what?"

"Don't know." She told him about a book she'd read this in in high school called *Sperm Wars*, which she'd found in the lost and found of the Pahrump town pool, where she'd been a lifeguard. Rose hadn't thought of *Sperm Wars* in twenty years. "It was all about the science of sperm and the evolutionary advantage of infidelity, what happens with the sperm once it's in a vagina."

"What happens?" asked the young Marine. Cade from West Texas, Rose found out later.

"What happens, if I remember right, is the sperm band together."

"Like an army," he said.

"That's right," she said. "Exactly like an army. All the sperm from the same man know each other, and they *work together* to get to the egg. If there's other sperm in there, they will organize and fight the sperm from the other guy to get there. They actually perform a lot better if there's another man's sperms in there. And if the sperm is novel, new to the vagina—"

"I know what *novel* means."

"Sorry. They—the novel sperm—have a way better chance of getting to the egg. So, like, you're way more likely to conceive with a random hookup than your regular partner. Isn't that fascinating?"

Cade said it was, his neck turning red.

"And what I think we have to ask, once we know this," Rose continued, "is why monogamy? Like, America is so obsessed with survival of the fittest and all that—"

"Social Darwinism," Cade said.

"Yes. And *yet*! There is no free market of the vagina. Why all these outward displays? If we really believed in 'may the best man win,' wouldn't we get a bunch of men up in there and let them have at it? But we don't. Monogamy is a vagina monopoly."

Cade took a slow, sensual drag on his cigarette and drawled, "Sounds like you're into trickle-up economics."

So they had sex. From what Rose remembered later, the coupling was completely adequate, physically. No unwelcome weirdness, no surprise violence, no squeamishness about the last dredges of her menses. They used a condom; he came, she didn't. Cade was very big and strong, but clenched. Remote, as you might expect from someone being trained to kill in exchange for college tuition.

Sleeping with Cade made Rose miss Miles worse than ever. Cruelly, her favorite part of the encounter was the possibility that Miles would see Cade's truck bounding effortlessly down Arroyo the morning after.

She again resolved to cool it with the booze.

To Live Outside the Law, You Must Be Honest

Low as Rose was after the Cade encounter, she was onto something. There was a reason *Sperm Wars* had come to her when it did, in the lost and found of the Pahrump town pool, and a reason it returned to her now, twenty-some years later at the Rattler Room. Divine timing? She ordered another copy.

Sperm was easy to come by, her hungover research revealed, but not exactly a dime a dozen. More like fifty dollars per month for access to the sperm bank's catalog, then one thousand dollars a vial, multiple vials per ovulation, with most conceptions taking an average of eight rounds of ovulations. For an at-home insemination, she would have to spring for top-shelf high-motility sperm, and of course education level was an upsell. Shit added up.

What a scam! Rose was looking at thousands of dollars a month rolling off her like dirt rolling off Pigpen. American consumerism at its most flagrant, most coercive! Talk about manufactured scarcity. Human sperm had to be the most renewable resource on the freaking planet! Two hours immersed in the web presence of the fertility-industrial complex and Rose wanted to throw herself off a bridge.

Alternatively, a method that she came to think of as the Swirl was free, and it was fun. Vegas pornoculture was a jaunt away. Joshua Tree just a hop across the Mojave Preserve and positively brimming with the semen of the aggressively healthy and overeducated: artist waiters with PhDs, rock-climbing bartenders with degrees in philosophy, literature, law. Between the two reposed five massive military bases stocked with bright young jarheads and airmen who'd MacGyvered their way out of America's sacrifice zones with nothing but their wits, guns, and chewing gum. The Swirl appealed to Rose's hedonism, her frugality and anti-capitalism, was megabohemian and patently feminist. Hadn't Frida herself essentially deployed the Swirl with Diego and Trotsky?

To live outside the law, you must be honest. Bob Dylan said that. If Rose was seriously considering the Swirl, she had to have a code. She wanted it to be consensual and sensual. She wanted her baby to be conceived in an act of lovemaking but did not need to be in love with the Swirlers, nor did she need them to be in love with her. She needed to be attracted to them and to enjoy the sex. Ideally, she'd have orgasms, which she read increased the odds of conception. And also just to start the baby off on the right foot karmically. Health history and genetics were important, but not as important as spirit, essence, disposition, bearing, a man's way of being in the world. That was what all Rose's great loves had in common, Miles first among them. No sperm bank catalog in the world would include a donor's cloud reports. None of them would show you what had driven him to suffer through years of Chomsky and Kierkegaard and John Donne. You could not vibe with an online catalog. You could not commune with a vial. Rose wanted the process to include the wisdom of her biome, to feel their respective ecosystems agreeing with each other. She wanted to trust her gut. She wanted her second baby to come from a place balanced between intention and intuition, the way June had (albeit from a completely different angle).

This was not at all meant to insult the women who took more, let's say, established routes, but Rose wanted to create the conditions that would invite the specific being waiting specifically for her to bring it forth. Honestly, she hated thinking of the catalyst for the new one sitting in some freezer somewhere. She felt the spark should come hot off the presses of the testes, fresh-squeezed from the scrotum, that gentle dandling satchel, should be delivered to her waiting cervix via an orgasm, the most beautiful and (forgive her) natural beginning imaginable. She wanted that. It had never been easy for Rose of Sharon to know what she wanted, but she wanted that. She wanted it with her whole body, was deeply in touch with her desire as she had been only a few times in life, drawn to the Swirl more strongly than she had ever been drawn to any cause or lover, even Miles. The Swirl was right. Rose felt so in what Mary Austin called her sacred middle. *This* was the Goddess path Rose was called to walk.

Everyone is here now. What are you going to do with that?

Rose articulated her code. She would be honest, and she would be responsible. Responsible to the Swirlers, to the new one, to June, and to herself.

If you are lucky enough to discern your truest heart's desire, as Rose was, if you become known to yourself—if you receive a freaking revelation!—and you don't do anything about it, you shirk it or stuff it into the way back of your emotional storage unit never to be seen again, that's self-harm. Plus it will be seen again. That stuffed-away shit leaks. It explodes eventually, shrapneling you and everyone you love. And this was not just Rose's personal code. Any guru or sponsor would tell you the same thing. Rose was done hurting herself. She was done waiting around.

Rag Friend

Rose called Cory, a law student at UNLV who'd been advising Camp Yellow Pine pro bono. Living outside the law was easier said than done, he cautioned, brushing her up on her exposures and liabilities, the myriad ways in which the new one might one day be snatched from her. By the end of their conversation, Rose had to admit the need for what Chief Truckee called a "rag friend." She bailed on a planned trip to Yellow Pine to research.

As reward for Chief Truckee's service in the Bear Flag Revolt of 1846, in which John C. Frémont tried to steal Alta California from Mexico, Frémont gifted Chief Truckee a gun (the Paiutes' first) and, even more precious to Truckee, a "rag friend": a letter from Frémont pronouncing Truckee a war hero whose people should enjoy the privileges and protections afforded any other loyal ally of the United States. Truckee's granddaughter, Sarah Winnemucca, listened skeptically as her grandfather explained the miracle of the rag friend, more awesome even than the floating houses galloping atop the sea that he'd observed on his adventures with Frémont. "*This can talk to all our white brothers and our white sisters,*" Truckee told Sarah and her siblings. "*The paper can travel like the wind, and it can go and talk with their fathers and brothers and sisters, and come back to tell what they are doing, and whether they are well or sick."*

Sick, ultimately. Very sick. Truckee's rag friend had tragic limits, as US law does to this very day. Neither Truckee nor his rag friend could protect his people from the violence of the American legal system, which doles out rights like rations and ultimately gave the Paiutes bubkes. Original sins and ongoing failings of US law notwithstanding, Rose had to admit that a waiver (a Known Donor Agreement in legalese) would probably be prudent when executing the Swirl.

To get his rag friend, Chief Truckee had to rescue innumerable wagon trains from their own idiocy and serve as Frémont's wingman as the future senator galivanted off on a doomed coup. Today, there's an app for that.

Which physical and genetic tests undertaken by the donor will be paid for by the biological mother?
None.

Will the sperm donor be compensated?
No.

Are any of the parties legally married?
No.

Is there a second parent who wishes to adopt the child conceived by this process?
No.

Who is the physician that will collect semen from the donor and perform the artificial insemination?
N/A

Does the recipient authorize the physician to use fresh or frozen semen from the donor?
N/A

Does the biological mother wish to offer to pay the donor's attorney cost (if any) in relation to this agreement?
No.

Five minutes and five dollars later, Rose had a pdf of a Known Donor Agreement. A quick trip to the Copy Center Plus in Pahrump and she had two dozen rag friends.

NOW, THEREFORE, in consideration of the promises to each other, Donor and Recipient agree as follows

1. Donor agrees that the purpose of this coitus is insemination to produce a child or children.
2. Each party is a single person and not legally married.
3. Donor understands that he is giving his semen for insemination and waves paternity rights, if any, to a child or children conceived by sperm donated pursuant to this agreement.
4. Donor agrees not to attempt to form a parent-child relationship with Recipient's child or children.
5. Donor waives his right to paternity testing and understands that Recipient will not seek to reveal the child's paternity.
6. Each party acknowledges and agrees that the relinquishment of all rights as stated above is final and nonnegotiable.
7. Recipient and Donor agree that Recipient has relinquished any and all rights she might otherwise

have to hold Donor legally or financially responsible for any child or children resulting from the insemination.

8. Donor attests that he has no known sexually transmitted diseases or serious genetic disorders.
9. Each party agrees Donor shall not be named as the father on the birth certificate of any child or children born from the insemination.
10. Each party acknowledges and agrees that she or he signed this agreement voluntarily and freely of her or his own choice without any duress of any kind whatsoever. It is further acknowledged that each party understands the meaning and significance of each provision of this agreement.
11. There are no promises, understandings, or agreements between the parties, other than those expressly stated in this agreement.
12. This agreement shall be construed under, and in accordance with, the laws of the state of Nevada.

Now to find some viable candidates. For that, more apps.

Contrary to the old siren trip—the witches, the Eves, the Liliths, the qi vampires, the vaginas dentatae, man's primitive fear of the disappeared penis, all the dumb myths and intimacy blocks she had long mistaken for mystery, chemistry, coolness—Rose discovered the digital dating world brimming with men willing to inseminate her. Too willing. Particularly middle-aged divorced men. "Father of your child" was a phrase popular with this demographic.

"Not exactly," she'd message. It seemed they couldn't hear her. The words were marked read, but the meaning wasn't sinking in.

Perhaps she was on the wrong apps. Rose expanded to CowboySingles, FarmersOnly, RanchersD, RuralMingle, and AnimalStyle. To her delight she discovered an app just for making a baby, JustABaby, but unfortunately it was only operational in the UK. She had high hopes for an offshoot of It's Just Lunch called It's Just Drinks and Breakfast, but found that set overprofessionalized, risk-averse, and neurotic. She perused the kink community and the dark parts of Craigslist, entertaining an orgy before deciding nah. Everyone wanted to film it.

An ovulation window opened and closed with no Swirl by the time the post office deigned to deliver a slip indicating the arrival of *Sperm Wars*. Rose immediately rode down to the Triangle and retrieved the book, peace in her heart for the sourpuss postmistress. Rereading *Sperm Wars* at the Rattler Room, Rose learned that *a woman's body allows sperm to remain fertile for no more than five days after being deposited inside her* and that *sperm seem to need about two days inside the female to reach peak fertility*. For her trickle-up economics to work, Rose would have to have a bunch of sex with multiple men many times over many days. Hot, but taxing logistically. This bohemian scheme was going to need to be executed with military precision.

She bottomed out on the apps. The apps eroded her faith in her fellow man. We were not meant to sift through potential mates at scale. Scale was not life-affirming. The Swirl required a degree of recurrence, a mutualism and reciprocity no algorithm would ever solve for. She deleted the apps, resolved to get proximate, began a local, humanly proportioned search for sperm in earnest by looking about her and deploying a process of elimination.

Not Miles. Too painful, too confusing, and he was no doubt unwilling. Rose didn't even want to tell him about the Swirl. It was no longer any of his beeswax, the comings and goings of her cervix. The Swirl was not a fantasy. Rose was not playing.

Pastor Jack was sweet and near, but way too old, and Rose was not at all attracted to him.

Cade was too young, had his whole life ahead of him, assuming he stayed upwind of those toxic burn pits the Marines so loved.

Rose sipped soda water at all three bars in the basin to get a feel for the male specimens at each. The Virginian in Tecopa Hot Springs was a favorite of fascist real-estate developers. The Crowbar in Shoshone was overlit and stocked with sanctimonious birders from Seattle. The Rattler Room was just right.

"Tell me your plan again," Lalo said, rolling a joint on the patio.

"I use an ovulation calculator to determine my fertile window." Rose showed Lalo the app and her journal, its moon glyphs indicating PMS, menstruation, and ovulation. "And basically I just fuck as many men as possible during that window without protection."

"Trap 'em," Lalo said approvingly.

"No, no, no. Just the opposite. I'm being completely open. Practicing radical honesty." She emptied the contents of her tote bag onto the picnic table: manila folder of rag friends, pens, prenatal vitamins, lube, chapstick. She handed Lalo a rag friend. "It's all aboveboard."

Lalo looked it over as she rolled the joint. "Seems complicated."

"It's actually really simple. It's the old way. Ancient. Pagan. This is how it was done before Judaism came along and made God a bad dad."

"Monotheism," someone said. A Black guy smoking and reading a book at the next table over. "Desert invention."

Lalo, daubing the tip of her tongue along the glue strip of her rolling paper, said, "What?"

Rose said, "Imagine an army conquers your village."

Lalo said, "What village?"

"Like an old-ass village in ancient times!" Rose said.

"Sumer, say," said the guy, putting down his book. *The Stranger.* "Folks with the cuneiform."

"I'm sorry," Rose said. "What's your name?"

"I'm B—" He scooted over and shook her hand.

Good shake. Rose's biome was intrigued. "Bilbao?" she tried.

"Below?" Lalo ventured. "Bilbo?"

"Bi*lal*," he said, "B-I-L-A-L. Arabic. Bilal Muhammad. My dad was Muslim. Means to moisten." Apt, for he was gorgeous.

"The Sumerians," Rose said, "yes, thank you, Bilal."

He shrugged. "I'm a prehistorian."

"So you know from whence you speak! By all means, help me out here. The Sumerians . . ."

"They invented writing?" Lalo said.

"Yep," said Bilal, snuffing out his cigarette in Rose's ashtray. "But before that, the Sumerians were Goddess people."

"Matriarchy," Rose interrupted.

"Not exactly," Bilal said. "Matriarchy is patriarchy's version of it. That's the first thing we must remember when studying the Goddess cults: We only have the victors' history, the men's words for it. When one culture overtakes another, either by violent or peaceful means—and usually it's a mixture of both—the conquering people absorb the positive or useful aspects of the conquered culture so wholly that those elements eventually seem to be their own, leaving the conquered culture husks of negative associations, misrepresentations, caricatures. These Goddess societies were matri*lineal* in most cases, female-exalting, certainly. But that doesn't necessarily mean women *above* men. We don't see that way of relating, actually. No oppression. No archeological evidence of warfare, weaponry, no money."

"No money!" Lalo exclaimed, standing and tucking the joint behind her ear. "What then?"

"Lots of art," Bilal said, "lots of feasts. In terms of structure if anything they were anarchic, no hierarchies: Men, women, plants, animals, rocks, water, earth, sky—these were not parts, not above and below. The same thing."

"All one," said Lalo, emptying one ashtray into another. "Like the hippie soap says."

"*Exactly,*" Bilal said. "It's a testament to our hunger for the Goddess how much of her remains intact and with us today, given the course of Western civilization."

"Like porn," Rose said.

Bilal frowned. "Not porn," he said. "I'm thinking yoni worship, womb orgasm, Black girl magic, certain Afro-feminist or Orientalist elements of the new New Age, yoga nidra, that sort of stuff. Commercialized, sure. This being America. Philosophically incoherent when presented in a market context. Sadly, apparently fairly toothless politically."

"For now," Rose said.

"But the vestiges are there. Triangles, pyramids, psychedelic art, the spiral motif, which we first see in the chthonic snake temples at Crete. Given what she's been subjected to, that so much of the Goddess is still with us is just *astounding.* And most importantly, in my book"—Rose had the impression he was talking about an actual book—"we see her lasting influence in whatever positive attitudes we have toward death."

"The Goddess is down with death?" Lalo asked, settling in beside Rose.

Bilal nodded. "*Very* down with it. Sees it as a cycle. Birth, death, rebirth."

"Like menstruation," Rose said. "'I wound and I heal. I kill and make whole.'"

Lalo retrieved the joint from behind her ear and lit it. "The OG clock."

"OG clock, OG paint, OG medicine," Bilal went on, teacherly. "In Crete the priestesses would guide women through menstruation, conception, labor, nursing *and* perform the funeral rites, all in the same temple. She'd lead the dead into the underworld. Similar thing in Malta, in Cyprus. In Çatalhüyük—Turkey," he clarified, seeing their faces, "the priestess slept with their bones under her bed. After the vultures picked them clean, of course." He laughed at his own joke, then got serious. "Then came writing. Big mistake, in hindsight. With writing you get literacy, law, debt, hierarchy, property, marriage as a weapon of war."

"Hold up," said Lalo, exhaling a skunky plume.

"O yes," Rose said.

Bilal nodded solemnly. "Some scholars do surmise that marriage was patriarchal religion's incentive to power via state-sanctioned violence against women in an alliance intended to suppress the resistant Goddess worshippers. Certainly, we can say, I think, that these early warlike protostates used marriage to *assimilate* the followers of the Goddess—"

Lalo offered him a puff and he took it.

"To capture her!" Rose said, then took a hit herself. "To co-opt her!"

"To neuter her," said Lalo, "and absorb her people?"

"That's why," Bilal said, "when you think about it, the women of Christianity make no sense. Eve? What's her deal? Lilith? They're earth goddesses whose stories are being interpreted by male sky god insecurities. Wielded for the purpose of man's political power."

"Like the Virgin Mary!" Rose crowed. "I'm supposed to believe she's some sort of goddess, but she doesn't get to fuck. The only reason they even let her go to heaven was because she kept showing up on tortillas and shit in Mexico."

"The Assumption. 1950, I believe," Bilal concurred. "And Mary Magdalene, or Miriam of Magdalene?" He whistled.

"The prostitute," Rose said, nodding.

"No!" cried Bilal, flailing his hands to the sky. "No evidence for that in the four canonical gospels. Mary Magdalene being a prostitute was some pope's idea way later. He said, 'This Miriam Magdalene is that Mary from this other book who was a prostitute,' just based on the fact that she, Miriam, had these seven demons released from her, more than anyone else. And those seven 'demons,' which later become the seven deadly sins, are probably not even demons. More likely they're related to the chakras. So you got the Eastern thread wove in. We could just as easily and probably more accurately interpret Mary Magdalene's seven demons as her being more enlightened, more healed, than any other disciple."

"Because of the chakras?" Rose asked, feeling for hers.

"And because who is it who first finds Jesus resurrected and tells everyone?" He did not wait for an answer. "Mary fucking Magdalene. And why is she 'moved' to go visit the tomb in the first place?"

"Because she loved him," Rose said. "Because they loved each other."

"Yes, that. That's important. Because there is evidence—we see this in her gospel and elsewhere—reason to believe that Jesus told her stuff he never told anyone else. That she was privy to his deepest teachings. Because thinking actually takes two people. And also, I think, she goes to the tomb because she's ready for it. She's spiritually *there*. She has her unguent—"

Lalo said, "Her what now?"

"Oil, ointment—most contemporaneous depictions show her holding a jar or cask of some sort. Preparing the dead. It's likely she was a priestess from an Isis cult."

Lalo exhaled another cloud. "Probably Jesus learned a thing or two from her."

"O yes," Bilal said. "Their souls were pressed together for sure. And remember: It is *she* who receives the vision of the risen Christ. And when she does, what does he say? Not 'Don't touch me,' the Western translation, which patriarchy takes as evidence that she's—"

"A dirty whore," Rose said.

"Evil," Lalo said.

"But that makes no sense, right?" Bilal said. "Because Jesus has healed her. He's released these seven demons. If that were true, if she were somehow contaminated, *evil,* Jesus would be bad at his job. What he says is better translated, *I think,* as 'Don't cling to me.' Don't grasp. Don't chase. Like, hold lightly babe. I'm on some other shit."

"I didn't even know Mary had a gospel," Rose said. "It's a Gnostic?"

"Before the Gnostics, even. Found hers in a clay jar in Egypt in the 1890s." He took another hit. "Short little gospel," he said through held breath, "about twenty pages."

"What does it say?" Rose had never really cared about Christianity before—that's not true, she'd cared enough about it to hate it. Rose considered Christianity's primary social function to be enabling and justifying the gravest harms of men and then shielding them from accountability. But now, slurping the last of her seltzer, she was intrigued.

Lalo too was riveted. Rose had never seen her sit still so long. "Any new stuff from Jesus in that jar?" Lalo said.

"O yes," said Bilal. "Quite a bit of new stuff from Jesus. He told her many secrets. Even the other apostles acknowledge this. Peter was *super* jealous: How was it possible he told her all these secrets? Did he love her more than us? Must we change our customs?"

"What customs?" Rose asked at the same time Lalo asked, "What secrets?"

"The text is fragmented, unfortunately. The first six pages are missing, big chunk gone from the middle. But the big thing he says is"—Bilal took a swig of his beer for effect—"'There is no sin.' His exact words to her! 'It is you who make sin exist.' Not as in Eve, not all evil serpent woman, but, like, sin is a mistake of perception. There's no fall to be redeemed, and women are certainly not to blame for it. We're all imperfect, but that doesn't mean we deserve punishment."

"What else?" asked Lalo.

"Well, right in the beginning, which is, like, seven pages in, Mary asks Jesus, 'What is matter? Will it last forever?'"

"Yes," Rose said.

Bilal flashed her a gallant smile. "That's exactly what he says: All elements of nature are interwoven, united. 'Everything returns to its roots,' he says. Which could very well be him saying, 'Babe, you were right.' Because get this: When Jesus is risen, Mary Magdalene isn't like, 'What's this shit?' She's actually pretty unfazed. More like, 'O it's that shit we talked about. That cycle shit. That between-heaven-and-earth shit.' Jesus even comments on it. 'You are blessed, for the sight of me does not disturb you.' It's Mary who first believes him, and explains the whole deal to the others, to Thomas, to Andrew, so they can get with it. She tells them how to proceed. *She's* the first apostle. More than that, some scholars suspect she was meant to be a coequal founder, the Goddesshead, Jesus the right hand, Mary the left. But they *squashed* her! We squashed her."

"That explains it." Lalo whistled. "You a chili man?"

"Is it by chance vegetarian?"

"Leaf eater?"

"Yes, ma'am," he said apologetically.

"Me too. It's vegan."

"In that case," Bilal said, "please."

To Rose, Lalo said, "Want some, darlin'?" Rose did. Lalo scooped up the ashtray with their roach and the pile of ash and butts she'd amassed and disappeared. Rose told Bilal her name, the whole thing, *Grapes of Wrath* reference and all.

He said, "Is she the one who . . ."

"The breastfeeding, yeah. Which is why you can call me Rose." They talked about Steinbeck, and the stunning stuff the sky was up to. Lalo delivered the chili and winked at Rose. "I'ma leave you to it."

Bilal and Rose went on watching the sky show and bonding stonedly over socialist realism and the reemergent Goddess. "I don't even know if we can say 're-,'" he said. "She's been here all along—midwifery, suffrage, abolition, Stonehenge, feminist art."

"Frida Kahlo," Rose said, "Georgia O'Keeffe. My mom loved them."

"Louise Bourgeois," he said. "Louise Bogan. Judy Chicago. Ana Mendieta. Goddess worship got Ana Mendieta thrown out a window."

Rose nodded. "Burned at the stake all right."

"Domination's no joke. *And still*, you see her everywhere."

"The woo-woo influencers in Joshua Tree, they're all rock worshippers," Rose said. "And those rocks are plainly pregnant. Why else would the boys so desperately need to climb them?"

"Many Native people thought so," said Bilal. "Mount Tam. Taos Mountain. Lots of the sacred places in Southern California too are super vulvar formations. Pussy rocks, if you will."

"I will."

Bilal had a strong, gentle bearing, very clean nails, effortless style, sparkly brown eyes with which he made ravenous eye contact. Rose learned he had a nine-year-old son who went back and forth between the boy's mom's in Tucson and Bilal's in Claremont, where Bilal was a professor at Pomona College. Rose liked best the way he talked about his son and his son's mom, his awe of her parenting skills, her patience, his deep gratitude for her.

"Would you do it again?" she asked.

He inhaled mightily and exhaled. "I don't even know what that means. It's the hardest thing I've ever done. And I have it easy."

"I don't think you have it easy," Rose said. She told him about Juniper.

"Shit's hard," he said when she finished. "Being grown."

Rose sighed. She felt she might cry. "Yeah."

"But this plan of yours"—he nodded to her manila folder on the table—"I think it's hella brave."

"You don't think I'm crazy?"

"Nah," he said. "Waiting around for permission is what's crazy. Waiting on unhealed people to validate your truth. Ignoring a call? *That's* crazy. This . . ."

"Swirl."

He looked into her eyes and smiled. Such a beautiful smile. "I'm down with the Swirl."

How down? *Down* down? Rose couldn't tell. She felt suddenly shy, said only thank you.

At last call, Bilal zapped Rose with another glittery smile. "When can I see you again, Goddess?"

Rose of Sharon got brave. "How about tomorrow morning," she said, sliding him a rag friend, "at a notary?"

Drop the Rock

Rose would spend her next ovulation window visiting Juniper. We need to say more about Juniper. One challenge is Juniper has no beginning—none of us do. Say she began as sperm slurped up by Rose's cervix and shuttled by an eager pulsing tube to a waiting egg Alice made. Say she began with Rose's legs aloft. With a prayer. With an hours-long walk along the Truckee River during which Rose and Will agreed to try one day. With the coitus after the walk in celebration of that decision. Say Juniper began after Will came and Rose came, after they slid sweatily around together awhile, after Will went to the bathroom and Rose swung secretly her feet to the sky, saying without saying, *Please*. That's what Rose believed.

Why not? It's as good a beginning as any when there aren't any. None of us have any beginning we recall, no start that we remember up top. But deep down, we all remember. We lived it. Our matter remembers being blown apart. Juniper began as star stuff, a fish in Lake Lahontan, lichen riding Pangaea. She began as her mother's blood, the minerals leached from Rose's bones.

None of us asked to be born, but Juniper was, on the last day of

October, Nevada Day, in Reno. She and Rose one being, then two. So Rose is forgiven for fearing she might never be whole. Forgiven for thinking it not possible to be away from Juniper. Rose *was* Juniper.

Juniper did not feel this way. She thought herself nothing like her mom. She thought her mom was a pretty good mom except she cried too much. Her mom was bossy and she yelled. She wasn't fun and she ignored. She was on her phone too much, brushed hair too hard, but always gave rubs at bedtime. She let June play *Minecraft* and be the DJ on long drives. She liked that. Juniper played Taylor Swift and Billie Eilish, mean and wounded girls belting their revenge. Juniper had secret names for everything. Her bike was Pinky, her mom's car Carl, Miles's car Donut, the trampoline Trampy. Her favorite color was maroon, her favorite place was the Borehole, her favorite person was her dog at her dad's house. She loved her parents and her iPad and her stuffies and her bedroom, she liked making jewelry and reading comics. She hated tests and rules and grown-ups who played dumb. She hated school except for recess, PE, lunch, and After School Club. She loved all animals, especially dogs, cats, bats, bunnies, lizards, and axolotls. She believed fervently in aliens, fairies, and Yucca Man. She refused to step foot in Joshua Tree National Park because of Yucca Man. She was afraid of the dark and of spiders, snakes, and bees. She was convinced without evidence that she was allergic to bees. She ate twelve foods and one of them was Brie. She loved the purple mountains around Tecopa and feared them. The mountains made her feel like there was nothing behind them. Like she was nothing, or almost nothing. A speck. Sometimes this felt good, and sometimes it felt scary. She knew she could never tell her mom this. Her mom had a special voice for talking about the mountains. Juniper hated this voice. Juniper loved her mom and was deeply pissed at Rose much of the time, for Rose had gone away and June had not known where or why or when she was coming back, and though June did not remember it up top, still it had happened. Still she had lived it. It mattered. They felt the separation between them every day.

Before reuniting with Juniper for spring break, before she'd be whole, Rose would spend a night at Camp Yellow Pine. Driving out there after a notary-and-eggs date with Bilal, Rose was joined by Jane, her dead sponsor, in the passenger seat. Rose could sense more than see Jane, yet knew she'd come as Rose first met her. Athleisure wear, blue hair, sterling silver rings on every finger. Rose could feel them clicking.

The time-striped Nopahs were aglow, the alluvial fans neon green with invasive grasses, their washes fuzzed with the promise of flowers.

"Pretty hard on your mom back there," Jane said serenely from beyond.

The Greeks and Jews bickered about whether such visitations came through the eyes or the ears. Rose's were more visual when she was younger, but mostly aural now, the intuition of image just beyond her periphery, a glimpse-sense out of the corner of her eye. She didn't know if that made her more Greek or Jew. She'd ask Bilal next time she saw him.

"Pretty hard on poor Chace too," Jane said. "King Boob?"

"Chace is fine."

"And how about you? A touch out of balance, maybe? A little out of whack?"

"Maybe," Rose admitted.

"Talk to her," Jane said.

"Let's not today, Jane."

"Come on, Rose. Dig in."

"I've been toiling in that mine my whole adult life. I want out."

"No way out but through," Jane said. "Free yourself."

"I've been through it, Jane. I'm angry, I'm hurt, blah blah blah. I've said it all before."

"Baba Ram used to say, *You can get more than one poem out of your trip to Rome.*"

"He didn't say that."

"Don't blame me. You're the one with the disorganized *nous*. Now, get into it!" she yelled. "Tell your maker what you need to tell her. Drop the rock!"

"All right, Jane! Jesus." Rose squeezed the steering wheel. "Mom: I'm mad at you. You hurt me. You abandoned me." Not just her death or the abandonment of her addiction, that oozing mother wound. "But even before that, the absence."

"That's what addiction is about," Jane said. "Nonpresence, the desperate need for absence, to escape your self. Finding the self unbearable and using whatever means handy to escape it. The addict simply cannot *be*."

That jived with Rose's observations. Alice could not rest, could not sit still. She couldn't sit with herself. She couldn't sit with Rose. Couldn't even *see* Rose most of the time. When she looked at Rose, all she saw was work. Alice was panicky, fragile. She made everything about her. Rose solved this by never needing her. "That was what I had to offer: needing nothing. That was how I could be helpful, by being needless."

"Tell *her*."

Rose grumbled some, then, "Mom: When I was a little kid, you made my problems your problems. You made me a problem. When I got excited, it was an emergency. Love was scary." Love was loss in the bank earning interest. Better not get your hopes up, was Alice's perennial philosophy. Getting your hopes up was the worst thing you could do. Hope was for idiots and tourists.

"Also, Mom, you loved foolishly. I'm not talking about the quickness. I'm not trying to slut-shame you. Anyone raising a little kid on her own while their beloved rots in prison deserves to be touched, to be held, to be loved, to make love, to feel lightness. To live. But after we got to the mainland—and, again, I don't blame you! I understand the economic angle! We were broke. You were raising me alone. I'm divorced now, you probably know, and maybe I don't have 'full custody,' am not the school-year parent, but believe me, I understand the appeal of the mediocre stepdad." In the end, Rose's was less than mediocre. "The man had no core. He had no center."

"He couldn't stand up to her," Jane said, "so he couldn't support her."

"He sure as hell couldn't protect me from her." While Alice spiraled, Chace worked, was at the casino or online. "And you picked this man, Mom. That's on you."

"Your mother had a bad picker. She never wholly integrated her loss," said Jane. "Never adequately processed her trauma, we would say now."

And so what? What poor, single, uninsured American mother was granted the self-indulgence of adequately processing her trauma? Rose thought of Alice's grisly childhood in a sacrifice zone, a girlhood of poverty and violence, of watching the bombs boiling in the sky north of her city. Rose knew about Alice's own nasty stepdads, and her being raped as a teenager, which Aunt Angie had told Rose about *en español*. Alice had never mentioned it. Following Jim to the Big Island, having Rose there at nineteen, the boom and bust, feast and famine of a drug dealer's life, the glamour and agony of being a martyr's wife. The chaos of the raid, which put Rose of Sharon in the system for a month, a time Rose did not remember and Alice could not forget. Rose did remember them going bankrupt from legal fees, remembered Jim going away anyway, remembered him liking it better there than at home with her.

"How could that be?" Jane asked gently. "How could that possibly be?"

Rose knew her parents' dreams had died on the vine, though she had no idea what specifically those dreams might have been. Only that she, Rose of Sharon, had killed them. But she had never asked to be born. "She was a person," she told Jane. "A whole-ass person. They were people. I get it. But what am I supposed to do with it?"

"*Do?*" said Jane. "Do nothing! Sit your ass down and feel it."

"My mom's answer to everything was 'Keep it moving,'" Rose had said to Bilal in Denny's that morning after their trip to the notary at Copy Center Plus, taking the scenic route in explaining why she needed their budding courtship to go tortoise slow. "She thought if she kept it moving, she wouldn't suffer." If only she could have chosen her suffering, sat with her pain awhile, been a little stronger, learned to trust herself. To be with herself.

"I know that's a lot to ask, Mom," Rose said now, rounding the hairpin turn above Yellow Pine. "I'm asking it. Of myself, I mean. That's what the Swirl is about. That's what Yellow Pine is about. I want so badly to be on this side of the threshold."

Jane said, "You want to *be* the threshold."

"Maybe," Rose admitted.

"What would it look like for you to forgive her?"

Rose rolled her eyes.

Jane hollered, "In all our affairs, muthafucka!"

Rose laughed.

"Try, Rose. Tell her. Say what you need to say."

"No, thanks, Jane."

"Do it ho'oponopono: *I love you. I'm sorry. Please forgive me. Thank you.*"

"I'm freaking sorry, okay, Mom?" Rose bellowed. "Please forgive me for . . ." She breathed deep, dug in. "Not understanding you. Not trying harder to know you. Being an ingrate. I *am* grateful to you. For all your . . . flaws"—not to mention the whole deck of late capitalism stacked against her—"you gave me a lot. So much. My life! Everything I'd die for today comes right from you. And it wasn't all a white-trash pain parade."

Alice had bought them the double-wide in Pahrump, on the north end of the valley near the mesquite dunes where the burros roamed. They'd had good times there, before the house was taken. The pink bathtub. The flowered wallpaper in the bathroom. Alice got health insurance through her union when she worked on the Strip. Rose went to the dentist once. She got glasses. She was loved. She was.

"And you gave me this land," to the extent that it was hers to give. Gave its story as she knew it. Driving to Vegas for groceries, to camping trips in Zion, Death Valley, Valley of Fire, Lone Pine, Mary Austin's house in Independence, Alice read Rose of Sharon the land. She named the mountains and valleys so Rose might know them. She told her how they came to be. This range, this fault, this layer of ash all the way down from a volcano in Yellowstone, this ancient lake nearly drained. Alice yarned in geologic time as good as John McPhee. How annoying it must've been to Alice when Rose started worshipping him in college. *I've been telling you this shit for years!*

"I used to wish I had listened to her more," Rose told Jane. "Now I think I did listen, in my way." Knowing a place was deeper than knowing its names. Rose heard Alice's stories, took them in, put them somewhere deep and secret. She lived them.

"And you taught me how to protest," Rose said, thinking suddenly of Memorial Day of 1996. Rose was twelve, Alice in a sober period. She'd taken Rose, with her sponsor and the sponsor's goddaughter, to join the Timbisha Shoshone, the Alliance to Protect Native Rights in National Parks (Rose looked it up later) and Greenpeace for a march on Death Valley National Park headquarters in Furnace Creek.

It was there that Rose first felt the collective lift of getting in the streets, in this case Highway 190.

Rose would reach for that feeling again and again when all else failed, which it seemed to do with increasing frequency as she came of age. Hollering in a pulsing, chanting, howling mass through downtown Reno against the invasion of Iraq, flipping a double bird to the pro-lifers tabling on campus every morning as she walked past them on her way to class, the heady autumn of Occupy, dragging Will and then Juniper to various women's marches, gun-control rallies, climate strikes, revolts against police brutality. Standing in front of the gas station in Pahrump, making her furious marks at the guild, singing Woody Guthrie around the fire at Yellow Pine. Alice had led her to all of it. Alice was the one who taught her that everyone had something to offer. Twelve-year-old Rose of Sharon's offering on Memorial Day of 1996 was to get whipped at basketball by the Timbisha kids after the march, and she'd loved it.

It took a while, like everything worthy, but the Timbisha did get some of their land back. In 2000 they were the first tribe to reclaim ancestral lands from a national park. Not that it's all rainbows and moonbeams for the Timbisha today—latest Rose heard they had to buy potable water from the feds and have it trucked into their rez. And, she'd read in a tribe-authored tract at the Shoshone Museum, they were still not allowed to harvest mesquite and tule, forced to watch the sacred groves and springs they'd tended since forever ruined by US ignorance and neglect.

But they did win, that Memorial Day. Rose always forgets that part. That sometimes, it works. It was hard to see a negation, hard to count your victories when what was accomplished was saying no. Saying, Take a hike. Enough is enough. That mushroom clouds no longer rose from the Nevada desert, from the New Mexico desert, from the Kazakh Steppe, from any atoll on this earth. That there was not a nuclear waste dump at Yucca Mountain, or in Ward Valley, where the five tribes of the Colorado and their helpers stood up against US Ecology's plan to pour radioactive poison into unlined trenches above an aquifer leading to the Colorado River. That there was not another Ivanpah in the south Pahrump Valley. Not yet. It wasn't easy to feel the presence of an absence, but Rose had had a lot of practice. Alice gave her that.

But more often, Rose had to admit, driving out to Yellow Pine, it didn't work. The desperate festival of demonstration dissipates, the peaceful assembly disperses, and then what? You could say what you wanted—you could holler and chant and raise your voice in song with dozens or thousands or millions of others. You could scream yourself red in the face, you could petition and public comment and speak up at stakeholder meetings, and your country would smile. *Noted and disregarded.* You could organize, assemble, take a bridge or a highway, take pepper spray to the face, lose an eye to a rubber bullet, lose a pregnancy to a water cannon, and then what? The wheels rolled on. You could free speech and assemble yourself into oblivion and, whatever, vote. It didn't matter. This nation allegedly belonging to you, *of* and *for* and *by* you, chose violence every day. And you were supposed to thank it—to *love* it—for what? Not disappearing you?

"Are you thinking this Swirl will make you whole?"

"I am whole," Rose said. "Circling it at least."

"Let me rephrase: Do you expect another baby to heal your mother wound?"

Rose drummed her fingers on the steering wheel. Looked in the rearview mirror at Juniper's empty booster seat. She took in as much air as she could and exhaled an audible ujjayi breath. "It might."

Jane moaned sympathetically. "O, darling. What do we say about expectations?"

"Resentments under construction," Rose said. "But I'm not talking about *expectations,* Jane. I'm talking about hope for the future."

"I notice you haven't run this scheme by many mothers."

"I'm a mother, aren't I? Aren't I, Jane?"

But Jane was gone.

When Rose got to Yellow Pine, camp was gone too. The kitchen, the tents, Fran's teardrop, all gone. All that was left was the doused fire ring, a hole in the ground where the pit toilet had been, and the mizpah by the fence, toppled.

Rose drove frantically to cell service and called Fran. No answer. Joskie, no answer. Finally, Ira picked up. He told Rose to meet him at Cathedral Canyon. She pulled up beside his truck at Quehoe's grave.

Quehoe, pronounced "key-ho." Born mixed and clubfooted around 1880, Quehoe is often described as Nevada's first mass murderer, a superlative that clearly does not count all the mass murdering it took to make Nevada in the first place. Quehoe's mother was a Cocopah, his father was not, and legend has it that for this reason he was first an outcast and then an outlaw. He killed thirteen people, mostly people who were trying to kill him for stealing food. He was accused without evidence of ten more murders, blamed, it seems, for every act of violence that erupted across the Mojave in the first three decades of the twentieth century. He was Nevada's first public enemy number one, wanted dead or alive. A posse was formed in Las Vegas, led by a cop named Frank Wait. The reward for capture climbed to three thousand dollars, but clubfooted Quehoe evaded the law all the while.

Then, in 1940, prospectors in Black Canyon, directly downstream of the still-new Boulder Dam, found Quehoe's desiccated body in a cave surrounded by all his stuff. A cloth bandage cinched around his thigh suggested he'd died of snakebite.

The prospectors delivered Quehoe's remains to Palm Funeral Home in Las Vegas, and one of them, a certain Charles Kenyon, demanded the reward. One might admire Kenyon's sense of entitlement, given Quehoe had been expired for about a decade. The state did not admire it, apparently, for Kenyon's request for the reward was ignored. Meanwhile, several of Quehoe's relatives came forward to claim his remains for burial. Palm Funeral Home refused them all. The corpse lay at Palm for three years of haggling and lawsuits, accumulating debt until, according to the archives, Charles Kenyon and Quehoe's relatives "disappeared." A judge awarded the body to the funeral home, which threatened to cremate Quehoe and scatter him in the desert if no one paid his tab. Thus emerged a buyer with sentimental attachment to the corpse: one Frank Wait, former leader of the posse who'd failed to capture Quehoe, who'd since become Las Vegas chief of police.

Frank Wait bought the body and gave his nemesis's mummy to the Elks club of Las Vegas for exhibition at Helldorado, the annual cowboy dress-up pageant the Elks had started in hopes of poaching some of Tombstone's cool. Quehoe was kept in a glass display case inside a replica cave at Helldorado Village in Vegas throughout the 1950s. One year, the corpse even rode in the parade.

When the Elks tired of Quehoe, they sold him to someone who sold him to someone who sold him to someone. Eventually the body found temporary repose at the Museum of Natural History at UNLV, where it was exhibited until 1975. At that point, Quehoe was purchased by a retired Clark County district attorney named Roland Wiley, the mad architect of Cathedral Canyon, outside Pahrump, a mile down the Old Spanish Trail from what would become Yellow Pine. On November 6, 1975, Roland Wiley held a funeral for Quehoe. "Southern Nevada's last Indian" was buried on a ridge overlooking Wiley's open-air temple. Frank Wait gave the eulogy. A concrete slab embedded with stones spelling out QUEHOE marks his grave to this day.

Change is *one of the culture's most enduring misunderstandings about itself.* Joan Didion said that.

"Put your phone in your glove box." Ira said that. Rose did, and they walked down to the pulverized ruins of Cathedral Canyon.

"I used to come here as a kid," she told him. "With my mom. For AA meetings. Her ashes are here."

Ira lit a cigarette and said nothing. Fun facts about Rose's childhood or Quehoe's desecration were of little use to him now. When they got down to Wiley's blasted grotto, Ira turned to Rose. "I'm sorry to do this," he said, "but I'm so fucking paranoid right now. Are you . . . ?" He gestured to her torso.

"Check me," Rose said. "Go ahead. Touch me."

Ira patted her down. "BLM," he said after. "They're charging Fran fifty thousand dollars for digging the pit toilet. Plus a three-thousand-dollar ticket for going over the camping limit starting last month."

"Last month." When Rose bailed on them. "Jesus. I'm sorry, Ira."

"It's not your fault. She just fucking spaced it. We all did. We were hanging out. Happy. It was probably my fault."

"I should have been there. I'm so sorry."

"I'm just glad my mom got me out."

"Thank God for moms."

"She'll get Fran and Joskie out too. Though Joskie I guess has a warrant from some Occupy shit in Vegas. And apparently he took a dump in front of Trump Tower during the uprisings? Fran'll need a place to stay."

"She can stay at my house. You all can. You can soak. Rest. Rest will help."

Ira rolled his eyes.

"What are they charging you with?"

He took a long, medicinal drag on his cigarette. "Trespassing, vandalism, theft."

"The juveniles."

"Mom says they claim to have pretty solid evidence. Which I don't know how they fucking do, unless . . ."

Unless someone at camp was a cop. "Roy?"

Ira's hands were shaking. "What do we really know about Roy?"

"He's not a cop. He's a retired park ranger."

"A park ranger is a cop, Rose."

"But he's retired."

"From which park?"

"Death Valley?" She shrugged. "I never asked." A big gust came up, whipping them with dust.

Ira said, "Roy's old and white and no one knew him from before. He wasn't there when we got raided. Hasn't been arrested, far as I know. I haven't heard from him. Have you?"

Rose shook her head no. "I don't even have his number."

Ira said, "Jesus, I feel so fucking stupid."

"That probably wasn't even mesquite flour in those cookies."

Ira laughed. "No, it definitely was. I know my superfoods."

"Will you lose your job?"

Ira bit his thumbnail and nodded. "And possibly go to prison for a year. More if Nevada passes that ALEC bill."

"That won't happen," Rose said. "Most of the Valve Turners' cases were dismissed."

"Most," Ira said, exhaling smoke like a burst pipe. "Not all. This isn't fucking Europe. This country actively decapitates its left! We put nuns in jail for spray-painting a peace sign on Oak Ridge!"

"It won't happen," Rose said again. But what did she know of the future?

A Moment

The next day, Ira's mom and Cory got Joskie and Fran out on bail. They went to Nothingness Flats to rest. Meanwhile, Rose flew to Juniper. She picked her up from school and on the walk to their rental told June that Miles had moved out again. Rose wanted to tell her right away, to have time for them to go through together whatever hard stuff the kid felt. June had welcomed Miles into their family wholeheartedly, teaching him to play Uno as if she'd invented it. She loved him. Loved having a big boy to bounce her to the moon on the trampoline. Rose braced for Juniper's heart to break, but the kid was tough.

"Dang," Juniper said, stomping a cluster of crunchy leaves. "What now?"

"Now we're friends."

"Okay!" she said. They walked on. June made a balance beam of a retaining wall, jumped off, twirled. Then she stopped, remembering something important. "But I thought you were going to have a baby."

"I thought so too," said Rose. "I'd like to. But life never really goes how you think. And you wouldn't want it to."

"Why not? I would."

"No adventure that way," Rose said. "No tears, but no surprise either."

June rolled her eyes. "I hate surprises. When *will* you have a baby?"

"I don't know," Rose said. "Timing like that is a mystery. You let me worry about it."

"But who will be its dad?"

"I don't know. Sometimes a baby doesn't have a dad."

"Like they die. Like your dad."

"Yeah. Or they're still here but they aren't here. Like, they have a dad but they don't really have one."

"I have one," June said.

"I know you do. A good one. That's why I picked him."

"Kids need a dad," said June. "I'd be lost without Dad." She held her head in horror. "Who would make my lunch?"

"Kids need someone to make lunches, that's for sure," Rose said. "And they need love, lots of people loving them. As many as possible. But to make a baby, what you need is . . . more specific. Simpler."

"What do you need?"

They'd discussed the basic biology before. That was not what June was asking. "You need the will," Rose said.

"Whose will?"

"Mine, mostly. And God's. The universe's? And," she admitted, "at least one man's."

"O." Juniper shrugged, an effortful gesture from beneath her gigantic backpack. "Easy."

"Yes and no," Rose said. "Listen. I know you really want a brother or a sister—"

"Or a dog," June said.

"A dog?"

"Yes," she insisted. "You need a dog, Mama."

"Why do I need a dog? You're the one who wants one."

"Because you're lonely," June said.

"I'm not lonely, actually," Rose said. "Not by today's standards. I'm probably the least lonely person in America. Did you know we're living in a loneliness epidemic?"

June put her thumb in her mouth, a sign of deep contemplation. "Pandemic," she corrected around her thumb.

Rose said, "I'm alone a lot. Is that what you're thinking of?"

June nodded. "It's weird," she mumbled.

"Maybe so. I'm okay with weird. I'm not going for normal. I like being alone. I'd like to be with you more, but mostly I like my life how it is. There's solitude, and then there's loneliness. They're different."

"Well, *I'm* lonely," June said. "I have no one to play with. I want a brother or a sister or a dog."

"What about a tortoise?"

Juniper growled, said she'd consider it. They walked on in silence.

"I'm sorry you feel lonely," Rose said. "I like your ideas for adding to our family. But a baby brother or sister probably wouldn't be as much fun as you think. They can't do anything for a really long time. It would be years and years before you could play with them, and by then you might not be very into playing."

"I know," Juniper said.

"You know?"

"Yes." June booted a seedball down the sidewalk, thumb still in. "I know what a moment is."

TWELVE-PRONGED NO EARLY EXITS MENTAL HEALTH ACTION PLAN (ROSE)

1. Juniper
2. Cloud
3. Nothingness Flats
4. Tecopa
5. Yellow Pine
6. mountains
7. valleys
8. plants
9. hot springs
10. the Rattler Room
11. the stars
12. the dead
13. yoga
14. tortoises
15. coyotes
16. action
17. meditation
18. vibrational healing

19. the Deranged Sign-Makers Guild
20. Al-Anon
21. books
22. walks
23. kissing
24. eye contact
25. prayer
26. making stuff
27. naps
28. solitude
29. masturbation
30. God
31. the land
32. the universe
33. not-knowing
34. hope
35. wilderness
36. creosote
37. mystery
38. suffering
39. unforeseen joy
40. love (beginning, middle, end)

More Mizpahs

Rose drove home from Harry Reid International, beyond exhausted by the transition, more convinced than ever that human bodies should not fly in airplanes. She attempted to soothe herself with a grilled cheese, fries, and a chocolate shake from In-N-Out. The meal fortified her out of the Las Vegas Valley and into the Spring Mountains, but in the pass the fatigue returned, doubled now with salt, sugar, and fat. Her eyelids got heavy. The road got slithery. Descending into the Pahrump Valley, Rose had to slap herself hard on both cheeks to stay awake, an old trick of Alice's. She rolled down the window, trying to blast herself into consciousness with cold. The sun seemed stuck in its late-afternoon assassin's angle, and the road shot her right into it. She couldn't see a thing and rocketed into that unknown at ninety miles per hour. The other cars on the divided highway flashed and flared as she passed them. She managed the turn onto Old Spanish Trail, passed Yellow Pine and the busted camp. The road rippled, weaved through the mesquite bosque. Rose's head dipped into nothingness and snapped back up at its own intervals. She waking-dreamed of being in high school, memorizing a poem, *something something a creature, naked, bestial.*

Then she saw it. Backlit by the murderous, annihilating sun. A black figure, long, dark shadow crawling on all fours across the road. Gnarled in wretchedness. A devil, Rose's first thought. A monster. Surprising, since the only devils and monsters Rose believed in were people. The creature sprung forth from the poem? She pounced on the brakes, and Carl juddered.

As she neared the figure, it became a body. A burnt body. Someone thrown from a car. Bloody, clawing their way across the asphalt from some accident. But small. A little kid.

No. Closer now, Rose saw that she was mistaken. Wonderfully mistaken. The black figure moving across the road was not a devil or a child's corpse-to-be.

It was a tortoise.

Rose swerved, missed the tortoise, careened onto the gravel shoulder fifty yards beyond. In her rearview she saw another car coming. She spilled from Carl and ran back toward the tortoise, waving her arms maniacally. The other car still came.

"No no no no!" she screamed involuntarily.

Sprinting, Rose reached the tortoise. The car swerved, barely missing them, its driver gawking like Rose was psychotic.

The commotion had sent the tortoise into his shell. He was an old boy, so dark! Far darker than the tortoises she'd met in captivity. The intricate geometry of his shell coated in a rusty brown-black, painted by time, shellacked by the Spirit moving in the void. His scaly forearms, forelegs, and forehead made craggy snug walls against the outside. His claws were like dusty chert points.

Carefully, Rose picked him up—her palms at his plated sides, her fingers feeling the smooth cool of his under shell. She carried the tortoise in the direction he'd been walking, across the road and well away from it, into a gully, praying he wouldn't pee from fright, because if he did, it was very likely he would die of dehydration.

She could hardly replenish him with the dregs of her melted milkshake.

"I got you," she whispered. "I won't hurt you."

Miraculously, he did not pee.

To her shame, Rose briefly considered keeping him—how sturdy, how portable he was all balled up, no wonder he'd lasted so long!—but she set him down, free.

"I never thought I'd meet you," she said, backing away. "I know there's not many of you left. Sorry about that, by the way." The tortoise stayed in his shell. Rose retreated to a nearby berm on the edge of the gully and watched the old boy. For a long, long time she watched. The world went white-gold, rose-pink, violet with orange cloud ships rimmed with gray. It took a while, but the tortoise did emerge. Slowly, beaky face first, blinking and looking around. He regarded Rose. Then came his arms and legs. Arrowhead claws scraping the dirt, he slowly scrabbled off. Rose watched him go. *Squatting upon the ground, she held her heart in her hand and ate of it.* "I'm sorry," she said again, and, "Thank you."

The sun had set; the valley gone blue then black. Rose was on the right path. Shimmering beside her in the darkness, Alice knew the poem. She said, *"Is it good, friend?"*

"It is bitter," Rose said. *"Bitter."*

"But I like it because it is bitter."

"And because it is my heart."

Back home at Nothingness Flats, Rose found the Yellow Pine crew stargazing on the trampoline. It made her want June, made her feel empty, bereft of purpose. Or maybe overfull of it. All this space and nowhere to put it. Sometimes she worried it sent her on all these kooky side roads and made her miss the whole deal. Love was the whole deal, Rose was pretty sure, and she felt it for Juniper always. It was its own, the far-apart love, a love beyond daily contact and constant service, beyond PB&J's and bedtime stories, a presence beyond proximity. Distance without disconnect.

But the longing was always in her. The separation, OG agony. Rose always felt the void where Juniper should have been, and it always hurt. Most days she was psychically limping. No one knew what this felt like, Rose was sure, though she also knew that wasn't true. The Bilals of the world knew. Her friends on the trampoline knew. Miles knew.

The gang's spirits were high, even before Rose reported the tortoise encounter. Visitation or no, Ira could not approve of her intervention. "What you want to do next time is block the road with your car and let him cross on his own."

Cory and one of his professors had a plan for getting Fran's fine dismissed. She'd raised almost all of it online in any case. Joskie said Roy claimed he wasn't a cop and had only been away visiting his grandkids. Joskie and Fran believed him, Ira was unconvinced. Ira's mom had gotten Joskie's penalty downgraded to community service. "Picking up trash on the Old Spanish Trail." Joskie laughed. "What I probably would have been doing anyway if they'd left me alone!"

"What about you?" Rose asked Ira.

The case against Ira was thin, according to one of his mom's partners, based solely on some grainy new-moon surveillance footage.

"And your job?"

"O, they fired me right away," Ira said. "Whatever. Maybe you can get me a job at the Sierra Club. Assuming they don't already have a bounty on my head."

Rose said she was glad they were all so cheery. "But I thought you'd be blue." *She* was blue. Maybe turquoise. Bright from her tortoise encounter, her Alice encounter, but heavy with June withdrawal and sad about Yellow Pine.

"Blue?" said Joskie. "What's to be blue about? We're not in a penal colony."

Ira scoffed. "We wish this country had penal colony numbers."

"Blue about we failed," Rose said. "Camp failed."

Fran grunted. "I love you," she said, "but I reject that. The point was to watch, to witness, to say what we saw. To invite other people to watch and witness. And we did that." She reminded Rose of the op-eds they'd placed in local papers, the hours-long calls into the public utilities commission meetings, the grueling BLM Zooms, the postcard campaigns, and frenzied public-comment periods. She showed Rose some social media metrics on her phone, then an article in *Harper's* by a professor who'd come to one of their campouts. She reminded Rose of a series in *The Dusty Trail* that had made the Pahrump town council pass a six-month moratorium on industrial solar in Nye County.

"So we convinced five corrupt climate deniers to cockblock the libs," Rose said. "Big deal. What have we done for the people of Pahrump, for the kids there? There's no program for free solar panels on your house, no way to get a shade structure with solar put over your mobile home for free. NV Energy is out there—Warren Buffett—NextEra—Lithium Americas—Greenlink—Bechtel—PG and E—investor-owned utilities—Big Tech!"

"No, totally," Fran said. "There's work to be done."

"You can't do a thing like Yellow Pine with such specific expectations," Joskie said. "Action sets in motion other unknowable actions. It's a culture, not a curriculum. If you want to do something knowing full well what the outcome will be beforehand, go to Walmart."

"We did save some baby tortoises," Ira said. "Hypothetically. And if nothing else, camp stopped us from killing ourselves. That's not nothing."

It was not nothing.

That night they feasted. After dinner they lounged around Nothingness Flats smoking weed and listening to music. Looking for a lighter, Joskie discovered Rose's manila folder of rag friends. She told them about the Swirl.

Lying on his back on the rug, Ira said, "I'd do it."

Rose said, "Really?"

Ira popped up onto his elbows. "Hell yeah. What an adventure! And I've been kinda wanting to have sex with you since I met your plants."

"Aw, thanks, Ira."

"I got you," said Joskie. "Count me in. I love making babies. And I have to say, I'm really good at it. And what a gift to be released from the chains of paternity! I mean, I love my kids, but."

"But this is something else," said Fran.

"Exactly," said Joskie. "It's cool because it's new." His face changed. "But could I be its friend? I know we won't know who the dad is—I mean, if it's mine, the jig is sorta up—but I'd want to be the kid's friend. I'd want to be, like, around somehow."

"Me too," said Ira. "I'd want to be, like, a weird uncle."

"Or a godfather," said Joskie. "Would you be up for that?"

"For sure," Rose said. "Absolutely. This kid's gonna need all the godfathers it can get."

Rose's app and moon glyphs indicated she had about a week before her next fertile window. Against Cory's advice, the gang drove back to

Yellow Pine. Rose nailed her Ross Gay poem to a telephone pole, and together they rebuilt the mizpah, this time with rebar, bigger and more visible from the road. They put Fran's sign back up.

With this rock pile we draw a line—We honor the yucca and creosote destroyed here—We honor the tortoises—We honor the soil, the rocks, the lichen, the moss—We honor the kit fox, the birds, the insects, the human—We honor the coyote—We honor the cholla and the barrel cactus and the unknown—a sacred pact with the living valley—With this rock pile, we enter the new.

Driving back to Nothingness Flats on Old Spanish Trail with Joskie and Ira asleep in the back seat and Fran vaping up front, Rose asked Fran if she wanted to have a kid.

"Delia wants to," said Fran.

"You?"

"Don't know," said Fran. "I think no. I don't want it to have all my problems. But sometimes I think that's a fake reason."

"What's the real reason?"

"Fear, I bet." She shrugged. "Maybe that's a fake reason too. Sometimes I really want to. Like, just to know what I'm made of—to know what it took to make me. What would it be like to walk around knowing a thing that? But most of the time I want to break the law instead."

"You *should*," said Rose. "I'll bail you out anytime."

"That's sweet." Fran made a big cloud and watched it go. "You're the outlaw."

Rose's turn to shrug. "The law is dumb."

"And has a bias toward extinction." Fran made another cloud, and it was gone.

After a while Rose said, "I don't know if this will work."

"The Swirl?"

Rose nodded.

"Depends," Fran said. "Work at what? Conceiving? Probably! Conceiving a fatherless child? Easy peasy. Conceiving a fatherless child without suffering men's fear, insecurity, control?" She raised her vape to her pursed lips, eyes bulging with doubt.

"Not entirely without suffering," Rose admitted. "That's probably not a realistic expectation. But suffering with room for other stuff? Where we don't hurt each other all the time? No emotional minefields, no cascade effect, no death spiral?"

"A mature, healthy, intact American male," Fran said, looking in the rearview mirror. "A rare specimen."

"I don't need them fully intact," Rose said. "Not pristine. Just healed enough to do minimal harm. That's all I want. From them and from me. I don't need perfection."

"And you wouldn't want it," Fran said, sipping from the vape. "Perfect is boring."

She exhaled and looked out the window. Taking her medicine, she called it, looking at the mountains. "These forces," she said. "They've done so much harm. Like with Epstein—or Weinstein. Did you listen to those recordings of him? Begging, wheedling. Pathetic! 'Wah, I have an egg dick.' 'Wah, you probably think I'm fat.' It's like, I don't *think* you're fat, Harvey, I *know* you're fat. So what? Lizzo is fat, and she gets down with herself. Like, what amount of money and power will make you stop hating yourself? None. It's bottomless. A Devils Hole psyche. The destructive force of male self-loathing never ceases to amaze me."

The women were quiet awhile, the land medicine all around them. Then Fran said, "But if you could find someone with an operational penis and testes who'd recovered from *that*?" She whistled. "Worth the search for sure."

Bilal came back to Tecopa when Rose's fertility window opened, as they'd planned. He picked her up at Nothingness Flats for a date, and she introduced him to everyone.

"Sweet little house of hospitality you're running," he said in the car on the way to dinner in Pahrump. Rose told him that Joskie and Ira had volunteered for the Swirl. Bilal was quiet. Rose feared he would bail, but she hung in there. If he bailed, he bailed—this was an at-will arrangement. Eventually he said, "I like it. Nice to have another brother in the mix. Creates some fruitful ambiguity."

At dinner Rose said, "I guess I have a type."

"What type is that?" Bilal said. "Wounded Thoreau sympathizers?"

"Convalescing desert rats on the mend with legal standing and adequate motility."

"Tree huggers of the Capitalocene trying to fix their inner issues with a bad bitch."

"If anything, they're fixing me."

"Nah," Bilal said, "no one's broken. Not *broken* broken. We're all a bit bruised for sure." He leaned across the candlelit table. "I've been wondering. Why this Swirl? Why not pick one? Abundance?"

"Abundance, sure," Rose laughed. "And apparently, biologically, a woman has a far better chance of conceiving if she's having sex with multiple men." She told him the stats. "Apparently every single one of us has an ancestor who is conceived from a sperm war."

"Pardon?" said Bilal.

"Sperm war. It's from this dumb book I read. I guess there are all these different kinds of sperm—assassins, obstructionists, egg-getters. Actually a really small percentage of sperm are egg-getters, the ones who get into the egg with the genetic material. Most of the rest are kamikazes. Which, yes, war metaphors are whatever. But the point is, I think, or what interests me is, we're here, all of us, because of struggle. And cooperation. An epic struggle and equally epic cooperation. And of course, this being a work of popular science written by a British man in the nineties, the book is rank with the ol' siren trip."

"The what?"

"Like, the myth of the feminine evil? Women always trying to trick and trap and confuse men. The sperm are absurdly overheroic, and he doesn't go at all into the grandeur of the egg, its strategy, its journey, its beauty, or the goddamn miracle of gestation! Not a peep on the glory of making a freaking being with your blood!"

Bilal laughed. "Word."

"And not a female orgasm in sight," Rose said. "But even just what all the sperm have to go through, with a few men in the mix, is amazing."

"The universe must've wanted us pretty bad."

"I think we have to think that," she said. "We come from struggle and we're here to struggle."

"Not *just* to struggle," Bilal said.

"But all the best parts come from struggle, the struggle we all struggle. To be here. To be whole. That's the taproot."

"And I think," Rose said after thinking, "that even though I've never believed in the One, I want to be the One. I was done with the whole love racket. Very 'abolish the family.' But then the last person I dated—my, uh, neighbor—he sort of . . . restored my faith in that project."

"The project of . . . togetherness?"

Rose nodded. "And family even. I think I'm ready to be One. For me, for June. And for this new one? Maybe busting up the dyad will make room for a new shape. Honestly, I don't fucking know. I get that it's bonkers. I'm just feeling my way through it. Trying to trust the mystery."

"*You are blessed,*" Bilal said, "*for the sight of me does not disturb you.*"

"Mary M.?"

He smiled. "She was all about that unknowing. The place between soul and spirit."

"I've been meaning to ask you: What happened to her in the end?"

"After her boyfriend ascended and his bros kicked her out of the cult? We don't know. We can't really 'know' any of this. The documentation—"

"I know, I know!" she wailed. "Skip the footnotes!"

Bilal laughed again. "A'ight! Chill. Some say she took off with a small band of followers for southern France. Lived out her days in the caves there."

"The Herzog cave? With the crazy period blood art?"

"Chauvet? Near there, actually. There's some good Magdalene cults down there who think she lived above Sainte-Baume, lived in the cave system there for like thirty years. They say she knew the caves so well she could navigate them without a torch."

"Because she was the torch."

He nodded. "And some say every morning angels would come and lift her from the mouth of her cave and carry her high over the forest and the mountains so she could hear heaven and earth singing."

When they got back from dinner, the Yellow Pine crew was stargazing on June's trampoline again. Bilal and Rose joined, sliding toward the others at the tramp's drooping middle.

"Look," Fran said, "the Milky Way."

Rose took in the smudged arc of it, harder and harder to see from this brightening rock, increasingly obscured by space trash, but undeniably there. It did not make her dizzy. Looking up, she was right where she was supposed to be.

The peace, and a throbbing twinge in her lower back, reminded Rose her window was open. She and Bilal had sex that night. He was quiet at first, in his head a bit. He eased in reverently, gentle in a way that did not assume her fragile. Soon he warmed up, asked a lot of questions, did she like it like this, did she like it like that? Did she want more of this, or less, or something else? A come-here with the fingers or an in-and-out? A bit of both? Fast or slow or medium? They both got there in the end.

The next morning, Miles moseyed by Nothingness Flats on a trash walk and, noticing all the cars, detoured up the driveway. Joskie said, "Hey, guy," and hugged him. Ira hugged him too. Fran gave a high five. Rose introduced him to Bilal, and the two men shook hands. They all had brioche Joskie had bought from the Kit Fox and pickles Bilal brought from the deli in Pomona that Leonard Cohen used to go to when he got a craving up on Mount Baldy.

"He a part of the Swirl too?" Bilal asked of Miles across the kitchen island.

"Leonard Cohen?" Joskie said. "I vote yes!"

"There's a relatively intact male specimen for you," said Fran.

"Except he's dead," said Ira.

"O no!" Fran cried. "When did that happen?"

"And how he treated Janis Joplin," said Bilal. "What did he say? 'I may have been a bit indiscreet.'"

Rose thought indiscretion for the sake of beauty should always be forgiven. Ira laughed and said obviously she would think so.

Miles cut in. "What's the Swirl?"

Everyone got palpably quiet. They looked at Rose, who jammed one of Leonard Cohen's pickles into her mouth.

"It's the swirl of emotions that comes with anything important," Fran said, bless her. "The way important feelings are actually a couple different feelings at once, mixed together. Always moving in two different directions at the same time, like in yoga, or poetry."

"And what peace is," Joskie said, "is the movement in those different directions being in balance. Not the same, not necessarily symmetrical—"

"Right," said Fran, poised to defend the asymmetry of poetry.

"—but in harmony," Joskie continued. "The Swirl is not just a tornado of confusion. That's something else. Like when you check your phone and you glimpse a fragment from the beloved—you are loved! Accepted just as you are! Seen and known! But then a freaking microsecond later—not even! Like, pretty much *simultaneously* in barely-upright-hairless-primate-brain time: Something awful, ugly, mean, scary—some *lie*, usually—gets shivved into that same secret place in your heart. You can't feel both as discrete, can't discern them. It scrambles your intuition. Puts your gut on the fritz."

"It's a pace thing," said Fran.

Joskie pointed at her fervently. "There's a right rate! For human experience to be marbled, for us to be able to enjoy the color of this vein, the contrasting color of that one. For the variation—the undulation—to become depth, dimension."

"To become beauty," Fran said.

"Compulsory velocity isn't beautiful," Ira said. "It's absenting. Diminishing. Dehumanizing. To space and back in a second? Gross. Big mistake, going that fast. Starting with the train."

"Some good things are fast," Rose said. "Some beautiful things. Love."

Joskie held up his phone. "This is way faster than love. Way emptier."

Fran scooped out the soft innards of a brioche bun. "Think how long it takes marble to form, real marble. Or even glass to cool. And glass took us for*ev*er!"

"This whole century has been a blurred colorless slurry of contextless intensity mistaken for intimacy," said Bilal, a shred of brioche clinging to his lip.

"Damn, Bilal," Joskie said, tapping his own lip. "Go off!"

Bilal shed the shred and went off. "The good gets tainted, hijacked, and the bad gets laundered in rationalizations, false equivalencies, cynicism. Gradations flatten. It's paralyzing, disorienting, meager. Bereft of imagination. Our nervous systems are out of whack and our moral compass is spinning around in circles."

"Like on *Lost*!" said Fran. "But is there something good in all this too? Like we've gotten so sick that we've—some of us, at least—had to get serious about getting better? Like after a near-death experience. A collective come-to-Jesus?"

Bilal said they were in a cycle but couldn't know where in the cycle they were. "We could already be coming round to something better."

"Maybe it speeds up at the end," Rose said. "Gets really hard at the end. Like birth."

"Things are picking up!" laughed Ira darkly. "And we don't know how fast it could get. No one talks about getting to high ground anymore. People wake up when their sky's the wrong color."

Miles looked shipwrecked. Rose too felt a tad marooned.

"The Swirl is also," she said to him, "my unorthodox plan for conceiving a child." She found her manila folder, handed Miles a rag friend, and watched with great anxiety as his gorgeous eyes ran down the document.

"Is it unorthodox?" asked Ira whimsically. "Or ultraorthodox?"

"Certainly it's ancient," said Bilal. "Primitive. Prehistoric. Also very futuristic. Postpaternity."

"Gnostic," Fran said at the same time Joskie said, "Rooted."

Miles looked up from the rag friend at the other men around the table as if he suspected them of radioactivity. "Can I talk to you?" he said to Rose. "Alone?"

They walked in silence beyond the plinth, to the end of Arroyo, around the corner past the wacky Villa Anita art compound and into the desert beyond.

"I didn't tell you because you bailed," Rose said in the desert. "Things got hard and you bailed. You bailed on us."

Miles gasped, stopped walking. Waited. "I didn't bail on us," he said finally. "That's not what I was trying to do. I had to stop because it wasn't right for me. It wasn't right for you either, you said."

"Parts of it."

"But that doesn't mean I *bailed*. I'm here, aren't I? Haven't I been here? There's nowhere else I want to be. I'm in your life. You're in mine. Not being your boyfriend doesn't mean I don't want to support you. I do want to."

"You'd think I was a crazy. Too much."

"I wouldn't. I don't think that at all. I told you in my letter."

"What letter?"

Miles's eyes got big. "You didn't get it?"

Curse you, George H. W. Bush! A hex on all you war criminals! Rose shook her head no. "What did it say?"

"I wrote it a while ago," Miles said. "It was an apology, sort of. Or more like a description of the problem as I see it. How I can be judgmental. Severe. Withdrawn. The apples thing. About where that shit comes from."

"Where does it come from?"

"Fear, basically. I don't know."

"Fear of what?"

Miles rubbed his eyes. "God, almost everything. Being here. Being with you again. Being a person. Existing. Going forward. Having a baby? Showing up for Juniper. Letting you down. You're so brave. I look at you and feel like a worm. And there's all this old stuff, stuff with my family. Did I tell you I've been talking to my dad again?"

"No," she said. "What's that like?"

"Confusing. I was saying in the letter that I have stayed mad at him, refusing to understand him, because I think understanding dissolves anger, and for a long time I needed my anger. But I think maybe I don't need it anymore. And letting go of that is related somehow to this other thing I was trying to say in the letter. Which is that I'm just in a lot of pain all the time. And I know you are too. And I know I don't know how much, or what it's like—" He started to cry. "And I don't know what to do with it."

"The pain?" Rose asked.

Miles nodded.

"Me neither," she said. "All this pain and rage and fear and sorrow boiling over. But other stuff too. Joy? I laughed so much with you. It's crazy how happy you made me. I would literally be like, 'Am I going crazy?' And I *was*. Maybe still am. Maybe it's crazy to be so happy when the world is so—you know. Maybe I made you into a god."

"Love does that sometimes," Miles said, "I think." They walked on. "Our problem wasn't something in you or not in you. Or me. It was in the thing we made together."

"I liked the thing we made together," Rose said. "It wasn't perfect, but."

"I liked it too. It was beautiful and I'll never regret it. But it couldn't last. I couldn't do it. I'm—" His voice cracked. "A failure."

"You're not—"

"Failed musician, failed activist, failed academic. Divorced. I drive a bus. I'm forty-three years old and I live in a van. I'm a drifter, Rose."

"You're not a drifter," Rose said, "you're an idealist."

"*I'm* an idealist?"

"And a rambler. There's a difference."

"What's the difference?"

"Everywhere you go you go on purpose."

"I don't know," Miles said. "I'm struggling with purpose these days. Feeling pretty lost. Maybe we were the purpose. I've thought that. Maybe it was just bad timing."

Rose said, "Maybe this just is the timing."

Miles said he liked the sound of that.

Rose said she missed thinking with him, loved how he thought.

"How do I think?"

"Like an only," she said. "On your own wavelength. You never do what everyone else is doing. It doesn't occur to you. I want to know what you think about everything—especially everything important. But this time . . . I was afraid."

Miles smiled sadly. "I don't think you're too much. I don't even believe in 'too much.' If anything, I'm afraid I'm not enough. That I'm not ready. Actually, I know I'm not ready."

Well, get ready! Rose screamed inside herself.

"I know people leap," he said. "And it's beautiful when they do. But I can't. Not now."

Rose said the good thing about now was it was always over. One day there would be a new now. Already it was here. "Does that sound crazy?"

"I've never thought you were crazy."

"Never?"

"Never," he said. "I don't get your decisions sometimes. . . ."

Ouch. Rose looked up to the cloudless sky.

"But I don't have to," Miles went on. "They're yours."

"Lately I've been realizing that I'm not as good at divining everyone's insides as I think."

"No one is," he said. "That's why we invented language. You're not a witch." He smiled, then sighed, some spirit swerving inside him. "Look. You can do what you want with your life. Obviously. But you can't make my decisions for me. If you don't tell me what I need to know to be close to you, I can't be close to you."

"I want to be close to you."

"Then you can't decide what I *would* do. You don't have that right."

Rose started to interrupt.

"And yes, I'm skeptical of rights, as a concept," Miles said, "but let's shelve that for now. I have a right to the truth of what's between us, and a right to my feelings about that. You have to let me have them." This was a way of being Rose had never seen in him, this courage. "And you're wrong on tree worship," Miles said. "Look at all they give us. Shade, shelter, fire, nuts, berries."

"Gin."

"Air!"

"I take it back," she said. "Tree worship forever. I'm sorry I didn't tell you what you needed to know."

"Tell me now."

"You heard it." She nodded up the hill toward Nothingness Flats.

"I want to hear it from you. From the beginning."

Rose took a deep and dredging breath. "Well, I guess the beginning is I want another baby. I've wanted that for a long time. Being with you again made me see that. Really know it. Know it deeply. It was hard to see what was what when we were together because I was so afraid of losing you. I was sure it would destroy me. But when we broke up again and the dust settled, I was, like, freakishly all right.

Sad, of course. *So* blue. I missed you. I still miss you. But I also felt weirdly good. I've been pretty okay since. Grateful, even."

"You seem great."

"I feel great around you. Around buddies. Even alone I'm good. Not always. But better and better as time goes on. I've got my action plan. I talked to Jane—"

Miles cocked his head. "Jane is—O."

"Been listening, praying, working the steps. Moving through it. Coming out the other side. I know what I want. I want that future I saw. I want to go toward it at least. With or without you. I know it's gonna be hard—so hard." Tears rose, made him a mirage. "But everything worth doing is hard, right?"

"Right," Miles said.

"And I know I can't even know *how* hard, or hard how. Even though I've done it before, I've never done it like this. I've never had this one in this way at this time. I've never done it alone. And even though a part of me knows I'm not alone—" She began to cry. "I also *am* alone? I mean, we're all stardust and whatever, and maybe death *is* just an idea. Maybe nothing means anything. But that doesn't change the fact that there's no one there. *Words can't hold me every night.* Lucinda Williams said that. The coyotes, the 'sotes—they hold me. I believe that. But I'm talking *holding* holding. Arms incarnate. There's no human here with me, by my side, not leaving. There's so much churn out here. Everyone blowing through." She wiped her nose with her shirt collar. "Except me," she said. "I'm not blowing through. I'm an earthbound creature. I can hold me at night."

Miles took her hand. "You're steady. Rooted."

"I'm here at least. And the new one is here. Cloud. Or whoever they turn out to be."

A storm of unease blew across Miles's face.

"Not all the way here yet," Rose granted, "like, empirically speaking. But who needs the empire? The new one's been here in my imagination for a long time. You and me, we talked them into being."

"I remember."

"And Juniper. Juniper isn't going anywhere. My love for her isn't—that's bedrock. Even when she's far away, I'm still her mom. That's the core. That's infinite."

Miles nodded. He'd reminded her as much many times.

"I thought you'd want to be left out of it," she said. "I was"—she wiped her eyes again and snorted snot up into her sinuses—"embarrassed. Afraid. Of what you'd think. I'm trying to be like the mystics of yore. I want to meet my vision courageously. But I'm just me. I do gloze. I do cling. Know what Jesus said to Mary Magdalene fresh out of the tomb?"

Miles didn't.

"*Don't cling to me.* Hold lightly. Nice to know they had a reach-and-withdraw dynamic too."

"I'm Jesus in this scenario?" Miles laughed. "I don't know how I feel about that."

"Be glad you're Jesus," Rose said. "Be glad you don't have to live out the rest of your days in a cave. Then again . . ." She told him about the angels.

"Not being your boyfriend doesn't mean I don't want to be here for you," Miles said. "To know you deeply. To know what you're up to. To help if I can. It doesn't mean I wouldn't want to be part of . . ."

"The Swirl?"

He smiled. That radiant, star-stuff, cloud-watcher's smile. He was quiet awhile, a sturdy quiet. Not a cloud's but a mountain's. It seemed he would do it.

"I have to think more about it," he said. "But I know you can trust yourself."

"I have to," Rose said. "I'm the instrument."

"And to not trust your instrument—" Miles said. "That's the worst kind of despair. It means you're always lost. Or using someone else's, which means living a life you don't believe in."

"I trust myself," she said, and did.

They walked back, quiet except to say hello to J, Carlotta, and the dogs at Villa Anita. As they neared the plinth at Nothingness Flats, Miles stopped beside a blooming creosote.

"I'm scared this will seem like bailing," he said. "And maybe it is bailing—I don't think it is. But." He fondled the creosote's oily leaves. "I have to go away awhile. Back home. Deal with my folks. Deal with myself, I guess."

Rose had never met Miles's parents, yet she'd always thought of them as hers. As grandparents for June and the new one. How she'd longed to be shaded by the upper boughs of Miles's family. But it wasn't going to work out like that. Rose had to go on with no shady generation above her, her tree lopped, the way they are in cities. She wanted Miles to take her with him. She wanted to pin him down like a bug under glass and keep him forever. Her heart said, *Don't move, don't move, don't move*. Her voice said, "Okay." She had to leaf out on her own.

Miles pulled off a sprig of creosote, mottled it in his palm, and smelled. "It's never been better than it is right now."

She had made Miles into God. And there was nothing wrong with that. He was God. He was God and he was Miles. God was Miles and Juniper and Alice and Will and Jim. Yellow Pine and the tortoises and the creosotes and the yuccas and the moths and the unknown. Fran and Joskie and Ira and Bilal and Roy and Jane and Pastor Jack and Georgie Boy and Ada and Travis the baker and the brewmaster and the whales and Lalo and Rose and Cloud and Rose.

Miles offered her the sprig. "What would you want my relationship to be, to the kid?"

She put her face to his cupped palms and smelled, accepting the 'sote's greasy terpene offering. "I'd want us to figure that out together."

"I don't know if I could not know," Miles said. "I don't know if—how—I could know you have this kid and not know if it's mine, or from me, or not. I think I'd need to know. I don't think I could live in that . . . mystery. I guess I'm not postpaternity. Maybe I'm insecure. I probably couldn't sign a, um, rag friend?"

"You don't have to," Rose said, amazed by the easeful feel of these words. "I'll waive it. Cory says it wouldn't be ironclad anyway. Given our history."

More sturdy quiet. "I have to think more about it." Miles sighed and inhaled from the creosote again. "I do know this," he said. "If you hear heaven and earth singing, you hear heaven and earth singing."

Ode to Alice

Alice always came when she was needed. She always answered when called. She came as she was. You always knew where you stood with her. Where you stood was keep it moving. Was don't get lost in the sauce. Was to live outside the law, you must be honest. Alice was honest. She didn't blow smoke up your ass. She did shoot the shit. She was against the bullshit and believed it the highest form of art. Books, she said, were the next best thing to sitting around a fire and bullshitting. Books got you back to the old ways. Like walking, like praying, like dreams. She worshipped them all. She left school in eleventh grade because of what her gasbag teachers did to books, she said. (Aunt Angie said she left for Jim.) When Rose came home from college and said novels about God were over, novels about Nature and Love were over, it was Alice who said, "Who says?"

Alice kept a cozy home. Space heaters and throw blankets she knit while watching TV, curtains she sewed herself. She was horny for Bob Dylan and Burt Reynolds and Thoreau and Ed Abbey and Melville. She was agog for *Moby-Dick*. Permanently installed in the glove box of her two-tone 1979 Ford Bronco was a plastic album of six cassettes wedged perfectly into six square molds: Burt Reynolds reading an abridged *Moby-Dick,* which Alice insisted they listen to on long drives.

And once Alice had breezed into the bathroom to read Rose of Sharon part of *Moby-Dick* while the kid was in the bath. The pink oval bath in the double-wide by the burro dunes. The flowered wallpaper. Daffodils and daisies. Little Sharon was nine, prepubescent, extremely annoyed. She'd been about to take a shot of bathwater from the gold-swirled cap of her strawberry VO5 and was irritated at the interruption. Then, for the first time, warm in the bath, pinching between two raisined fingers the golden shampoo cap chalice filled to the brim, Rose noted and denied her impulse to snarl at her mother to *Get out!*

This was new. It was cool. This was not the child's passive love, the force-of-nature love-feeling that needed nothing, that arose of its own accord, unnoticeable for its omnipresence. This was the grown-up practice of love, an action, a love-doing, here a not-doing. Rose grasped for the first time—an ephemeral epiphany—the discipline of love.

And Alice plopped down cross-legged on the bath mat. "Listen to this: *These smaller whales—now and then visiting our becalmed boat from the margin of the lake—evinced a wondrous fearlessness and confidence, or else a still becharmed panic which it was impossible not to marvel at. Like household dogs they came snuffling round us, right up to our gunwales, and touching them; till it almost seemed that some spell had suddenly domesticated them. Queequeg patted their foreheads; Starbuck scratched their backs with his lance; but fearful of the consequences, for the time refrained from darting it.*"

Little Rose of Sharon thought, Darting *it? A dog? Wait, a* whale*?*

Alice went on. "*But far beneath this wondrous world upon the surface, another and still stranger world met our eyes as we gazed over the side. For, suspended in those watery vaults, floated the forms of the nursing mothers of the whales, and those that by their enormous girth seemed shortly to become mothers."*

"Nursing baby whales?" asked Rose.

Alice nodded. *"The lake, as I have hinted, was to a considerable depth exceedingly transparent; and as human infants while suckling will calmly and fixedly gaze away from the breast, as if leading two different lives at the time; and while yet drawing mortal nourishment, be still spiritually feasting upon some unearthly reminiscence."* Alice looked up and smiled, eyes brimming. "That was you, stuck to my titty and taking in the whole world. *Spiritually feasting.*"

Sassy preteen Sharon rolled her wide brown eyes. Moved, grateful, water-soft, love-doing Rose silently urged her mother to keep reading.

"—even so did the young of these whales seem looking up towards us, but not at us, as if we were but a bit of Gulfweed in their new-born sight." Alice collapsed against the pink tub, spent. *"But a bit of Gulfweed in their new-born sight!* Herman Melville said that."

Rose of Sharon felt helicopters whomping inside her. She let the bathwater dribble from the shampoo cap. She wanted to know what would happen to the baby whales. It was a babyish question, but she wanted to know. "Do they get away?"

Alice regarded her daughter, astonished. Rose watched her mother make a difficult decision. "O, sweetie," Alice said. "No."

The Threshold and the Vessel

And so what if the bathtub epiphany had been ephemeral? Ephemeral does not mean extinct. It means to come and go. After her love-doing walk with Miles, Rose drove Ira and Joskie to Pahrump, to the same notary she'd gone to with Bilal, praying for knowledge of God's will and the power to carry that out. Joskie rode shotgun, Ira in the back opposite June's booster seat.

Bless that pudgy, nonjudgy notary at Copy Center Plus, his soul patch pinning down his chins, his zippered satchel with his important stamps and space pens and embosser, his peace lily thriving in the corner. A vast improvement on John C. Frémont, the friends agreed after. Joskie said it went beyond that, said the *Plus* in Copy Center Plus stood for grace.

Bilal and Fran stayed behind at Nothingness Flats and cleaned. Joskie, Ira, and Rose came home to fresh sheets, clean dishes drying in the rack, shining concrete floors, vacuumed rugs, wiped-clean shelves and counters, freshly watered plants. A temple prepared. Fran had left flowers, dyed daisies, which Rose usually hated but loved today. There was a note folded beside the flowers:

Dear Rose,

Thank you for welcoming me to Nothingness Flats. What a place. Sorry I had to split—I am off to see my family in Orange County, speaking of the Swirl. Gah! I wish you great success with yours.

You know when you're hiking and you've been out there a while, away from everything, and you see another person on the trail, how exciting it is, even though the whole point of hiking, for me, is getting away from people? I think it's because if this person is way out here on this trail then on some level they must be my kind of person. So we've found each other. I'm honored to have met you on this trail. Let's soak when I get back.

Yrs in the struggle,
Fran

PS: Dilly and I broke up.

Rose did a berserk little dance when she read this. Three cheers for transformation!

Miles came over with champagne, Fritos, and a present for Rose: his favorite thing he'd ever found on a trash walk, a rusted pink spring-like donut looped in on itself, without beginning or end. He got glasses for champagne. Rose got her and Joskie seltzers from the fridge.

"None for you?" Miles said, pouring.

"Been drying out a little," Rose said. "Trying to cool it. Figured I should stop resisting my matrilineage and try sobriety at least once in my life. I'm not being absolutist about it. I'll have the occasional toot of weed."

"Cali sober," laughed Joskie. He had thirteen years OG sober.

"I just can't get down with the whole 'falling off the wagon' mentality," Rose said. "That's a harsh metaphor around here."

Bilal said lucky for her, they lived in the golden age of bubbly water. "I would have preferred we decarbonized the economy, but instead we have guava seltzer and waterproof wireless speakers. Imagine what actual problems we could solve if we tried!"

Miles proposed a toast. "To trying. To the new."

They toasted. Rose took a sip of Miles's champagne, because matrilineage was not predestination.

They feasted on Fritos, cukes, hummus, dates from the farm up the canyon, leaves dressed with oil and vinegar and lemon juice, fig yogurt from the Greek at the Pahrump farmers market, apples Miles could accept. He went home after dinner; told Rose he'd see her soon. With Miles gone, Ira looked at Rose electrically. "Shall we?"

Together, and in shifting constellations over the next few days, they honored the human.

Ira was eager, a little jittery. He was funnier than Rose knew and made her laugh a lot. He came quickly their first time, apologized, then triumphantly recanted. "Wait, I'm *not* sorry!"

Joskie was surprisingly serious for a clown, went down on her forever, which was wonderful. Rose just laid back and received. *So this is what they mean by an abundant mindset.*

Bilal again. More vigorous this time, downright acrobatic. Holding her in the afterglow, he asked, "What's the story with this neighbor?"

"He's just a friend."

"A friend who restored your faith in togetherness."

Rose nodded against Bilal's chest, his heart beating in her cheekbone.

"So you're available then?" His voice so ardent. "Emotionally? Spiritually? Are you . . . free?"

"O." Rose knew the truth would mean Bilal was out. So be it. "No," she said. "I'm pretty much devoted to him."

Rose watched Miles's school bus chug contemplatively around town for the last weeks of the school year, waiting to see if the Swirl would take.

It didn't.

The wildflowers did, bursting in a late bloom from the lime fuzz on the alluvial fans, yellow clumps of suncups frothing the washes and the sides of the roads. Next came shaggy purple lupine and miles of mustard. Milky bulbous cones erupted from the yuccas and the Joshua trees, and red trumpets sprang forth from the pomegranate at Nothingness Flats. The oleanders went insane. At last came the burning-neon-fuchsia blooms of beavertails. You could see them a mile away.

Miles left for Portland. "Jesus, these flowers," he said, hugging Rose to him, saying goodbye. "Talk about resurrection. The purple and yellow."

"I love when they do that color-wheel shit."

Miles regarded her, shining. "I love you," he said.

"I feel it. It's never been better than it is right now."

Summer came. Juniper came. A time of extremes, simplicity, sustaining. Searing heat and blanching light. Siestas and screen time. Lessons in tying shoelaces, cutting strawberries, washing dishes. Hats and ice water, wet kerchiefs around the neck, aloe gel in the fridge, Popsicle happy hour, bike rides at sunset, swimming at the Pahrump town pool. Every summer for years now, Rose had taught

Juniper to swim—every year she forgot. It was a thinking problem, they agreed, not a doing problem.

Some of the high-profile climate heads started distinguishing in their commentary between industrial solar on public land and distributed solar in the built environment. The Desert Committee put out a special issue of the *Desert Report* on the problems of poorly sited industrial solar and the folly of sacrificing wilderness for green capitalism. HR hired Topher's replacement and invited Rose back to the Club. Instead, she quit. Sent her résumé to the guy from the Center for Biological Diversity who'd spoken at Yellow Pine.

Fran came through Tecopa on her way back from Orange County. She brought a copy of a major magazine with a cover story in which their environment writer, in a first for him (Fran said), called for solar arrays on expired ag land and parking lots instead of just, you know, wherever. Miraculously, the temperature fell below a hundred that day, so they went for a soak at sunset. Fran was a goddess at the Borehole, scaring off tourists with her naked tai chi. Juniper adored her. After the soak the three of them walked around picking up trash, watching the swallows swoop over the wetlands, then the kestrels, then the bats.

"I assume you're not pregnant," Fran whispered to Rose when June was distracted by the bats.

"How'd you know?"

"The soak," she said. "OG abortion."

Juniper bounded up to them, wildly swinging her trash sack. "Bats are the worst things at flying that can fly," she announced importantly. "Like, technically they can fly, but their fly is chaotic. Like, even they are surprised they can do it. I know, I know, they're using echolocation. But still!" She thrust her trash bag at Rose, then scrabbled up the clay hill after the bats and out of earshot.

"Will you try again?" Fran asked.

"The boys offered. I decided not to."

"Never?"

"Not never. Just not right now. Not this time around."

"You have time," Fran said.

"I do have time," Rose said. "Not infinite time. But some time."

Rose did attempt the Swirl again, once, with Ira and Joskie, late that summer after taking Juniper back to her dad's. Fun, but no luck.

Then, when the stars were in roughly the same position as when all this began, Miles came back to Nothingness Flats. New again, and older. Ready, he said. Every piece and part of him. Or enough of them, he revised. He was down to try again if she was.

Try again at what? Rose needed to know. "Conceiving? Loving each other? Making a life together?"

"All of the above," he said. "Or whatever parts you're up for."

She was up for all of it, the whole beautiful, spirally mess. She was the threshold and the vessel. Miles the lovingest piston overhead. Rose had several easy orgasms with him that night, was fantastically lazy throughout. No. Rose no longer believed in laziness. She believed in rest.

After, Miles held her in his long arms. They talked about what the sky was doing, about the Swirl, drinking, the Rattler Room, Lalo, loneliness, Quehoe, death, control, anxiety, drugs, Yellow Pine, the decaying empire, palm trees, euphoria, tattoos, canyons they'd known, wildflowers and climate models and atmospheric rivers and the Sierra snowpack, Mary Austin, the sacred middle, peace, doubt, Juniper, peace again, love-feeling, love-doing, faith, trust, the Spirit moving in the void, Jane, their parents, coyotes, *The Protestant Ethic and the Spirit of Capitalism*, hope, sitting-with, reaching-for, judgment, rejection, time, Whitman, Didion, Melville, mizpahs, Lucinda Williams (*I thought about you all the way from Little Rock to Houston*), fear, loss, rocks, God, how they'd never done this moment. Then Miles kissed her and said, "Again?"

The gospel of *Yes*.

After, he got them water. He put on music in the living room, some trippy jazz Rose didn't recognize. Somewhere, a tortoise tried to go home. Alone, sweaty, slick, and swollen in her spectacularly tossed bed, Rose propped her butt up on her hands and lifted her legs to the sky. She did not know where in the cycle they were. To the new one, she said without saying, *Welcome*.

She said, *There is a light in you. It was lit a long time ago. It will be in you the day you are born. I can't wait to meet you. I can't wait to greet your light. I'm sorry to say your light will be dimmed at times in this life, but know that it will never go out. It will always be in you.*

Everyone is here now, and we are ready for you.

Acknowledgments

Mary Austin's *Experiences Facing Death* and *The Land of Little Rain,* Ashely Dawson's *Extinction: A Radical History* and *People's Power,* Sally Denton's *The Profiteers,* Ben Ehrenreich's *Desert Notebooks,* Elinor W. Gadon's *The Once and Future Goddess,* Ross Gay's *Catalogue of Unabashed Gratitude,* Baba Ifa Karade's *The Handbook of Yoruba Religious Concepts,* Jean-Yves Leloup's *The Gospel of Mary Magdalene,* Kim Stringfellow's *Jackrabbit Homestead: Tracing the Small Tract Act in the Southern California Landscape, 1938–2008,* Joy Williams's *Ill Nature,* Sarah Winnemucca Hopkins's *Life Among the Piutes,* and Sally Zanjani's *Sarah Winnemucca* were touchstones for this book, as was the work of John Craigie and Birdie Hall. obligatorynoteofhope .com was made by Jenny Offill.

Fran's mizpah sign is based on a similar one written by Shannon Salter. Parts of what became this book first appeared in *The Nevada Independent* (with Shannon Salter and Ruth Nolan), *The New York Review of Books, The Believer,* and Wildsam's *Joshua Tree National Park.* Thanks to those editors, especially Daniel Gumbiner, who first sent me to Yellow Pine. Thanks to Shoshone Village, where I was an artist-in-residence while writing the first draft of this.

Thank you to the Protect Thacker Pass collective and the People of Red Mountain, for your courageous presence in opposition to lithium mining at Thacker Pass/Peehee mm'huh. Thank you to the members of the Five Tribes of the Colorado River and others who bravely protected Ward Valley and the Colorado River, to the late Phil Klasky for sharing that story with the Mojave Project, all of whom inspired Camp Yellow Pine. Thank you to all watchers, water protectors, and land defenders. Thank you to my friends and family who keep me intact.

Thank you, Yellow Pine. You are missed.